The Keeper of Things

The Keeper of Things

Susana Correia

Life Rattle Press
Toronto, Canada

Published in Canada by Life Rattle Press, Toronto
www.liferattle.ca

Canadian Cataloguing in Publication Data
Correia, Susana
The Keeper of Things
ISBN 978-1-989861-05-9

Life Rattle New Publishers Series
ISSN 978-1-897161-84-5

Cover Design by Katherine Mountford
Cover Photograph by Michael Hills

Printed and bound in Canada

Dedicated to Brandon and Katelynn,
my anchor and my life-saver,
who have kept me stable throughout turbulent storms
and afloat during the high-tides.

The Keeper of Things

Part I

Chapter 1   August 2016

I have often heard 'man is a horrid creature.' That he will cheat, steal, and lie if the opportunity presents itself. He will damn his own family in the name of saving face and fight a losing battle rather than admit defeat. Rather than surrender, he will choose death. As a result of man's wayward nature, people will cut you off in traffic, swear at you from the safety of their vehicles, and offer obscene gestures rather than apologize for their errors. It is in this frenzy of madness that I find myself this morning, seated amongst shattered glass on a cold tile floor, staring wildly at the chaos around me.

To my left lies an aged man. One hand is fastened over his chest as he grips the material of his shirt into a tight fist. Turning his head to one side, he reveals the fresh blood that has pooled into his ear. His lips move but I can't hear what he's saying. More distinct are the tearful cries of the young child gripping her mother's neck.

"Miss." A hand sinks into my shoulder and I jolt. "It's okay," she says. The young woman in the blue uniform kneels in front of me. Her voice is barely audible as she tells me, "We're here to help."

The paramedic looks me over, then points towards the doors of the café where her colleague aids the young girl and her mother. She calls out to him before moving onto the man with the bloody ear. Moments later, the second paramedic hovers in front of me. I tell him I'm fine, confused, but fine.

"Miss." He takes me by the arm. "Please, come with me."

As he helps me to my feet, a sharp sound pierces my eardrums. I raise my hands to my head, and that's when I see it, a two-inch shard of glass protrudes from my forearm.

The paramedic steadies my injured arm. "It's alright," he tells me as I look on in horror. "We're going to take good care of you."

Inside the ambulance, he works to secure the piece of glass into position. I wince and he tells me that he's almost done. Then, with a gentle hand to my shoulder, he says, "You're going to be fine."

That day, in the midst of chaos and tragedy, I came to find the worst and the best of man.

§

"That should do it." In the emergency room of the Mississauga hospital, a nurse patches up my arm with a thick layer of gauze to hide the twenty-four stitches and the dried clusters of blood. "The doctor will be in shortly to sign off on your discharge."

Leaning against the pillows of the narrow bed, I gaze across the hallway to a poem hanging on the beige wall. The poem is "In Flanders Fields" by John McCrae. A large red poppy covers the top half of the picture. There's something haunting yet hopeful in that poem. For all the soldiers lost, the families that have suffered through those losses, and those that have returned and remain lost, there is hope.

A couple of feet over another poem hangs. This one is titled "The Second Coming" by W.B. Yeats.

> *'Things fall apart; the centre cannot hold;*
> *Mere anarchy is loosed upon the world,*
> *The blood-dimmed tide is loosed, and*
> *everywhere, The ceremony of innocence*
> *is drowned'*

The words evoke a sense of mystery and leave an impression. Something awakened, something stirring…

"Issy." The deep, familiar voice breaks my thoughts and I turn to find Adrian standing at the open curtain. The sight of him brings a smile to my face.

In two long strides, he's at my bedside. His hands cup my chin while his green eyes study the small cuts on my face. "Are you alright?"

"Yeah." I lift my arm. "Got a souvenir though."

Sitting on the edge of the bed, Adrian takes my bandaged arm into his hands. "What happened?"

"There was an explosion."

"An explosion? From what?"

I shrug. "The police were here asking questions, but I didn't see anything. It was all so sudden."

What I do know is that the explosion occurred in a small ocular laboratory across the road from Rosa's Café. The impact shattered the windows of the coffee shop. Glass embedded into cushions and clothing and skin.

"That's terrible," he says, his lips puckering into an adorable pout.

My best friend, Adrian, is the most beautiful man you'll ever meet. Standing at six feet, two inches, he boasts a lean muscular build along with a handsome face of chiselled features. Coupled with those seductive eyes and waves of dark hair, he's a modern-day *David*.

Thirty minutes later, I'm discharged from the hospital. As we settle into Adrian's smart, compact BMW, he turns to me and asks, "Did you call him?"

"Why would I call him?"

"He'll want to know that you're okay."

"He doesn't know I'm hurt."

Mike and I hadn't spoken since our break-up of one month ago unless last weekend's unfortunate encounter can be construed as speaking. Mike entered Rosa's Café and I was there; I was always there. The problem was that so was Adrian. An altercation ensued, and Mike was escorted out. That is what remains of our four-year relationship.

Adrian gives me a hard look. "He's going to find out and he's going to be upset."

"I don't care. And how is he going to find out, anyway?"

With an amused grimace, he states as a matter of fact, "Your brother."

I sigh. Right, Eric. My wayward brother, my fraternal twin was as chaotic as the rest of society. He was always ready to tell someone off and just as eager for the next fight. But, more than anything, Eric was so unlike Mike.

They'd met back in grade nine. After graduation, Mike went off to university on a football scholarship and Eric, oozing with what I believed to be a fierce case of 'Superman Syndrome,' decided that he would join the Canadian military.

§

At eighteen years of age, although a tough kid, my brother was still lanky. Mike and I teased him certain that he wouldn't get past training.

"And what the hell are you going to do?" Eric shouted across the deck of our house. "Just sit on the sidelines and watch?"

"Damn Skippy," Mike teased.

"How convenient." My brother sneered at us. "But that's the problem with our over-privileged society, isn't it? Nobody gives a damn about what's going on just as long as it doesn't get too close to home. 'Cause hell, it's not your problem, right?" Eric stood up and, with bitterness on his tongue, he said, "Just like a herd of cattle, blind and arrogant to everything around you."

I'd heard enough. "What's gotten into you?" I snapped at him.

"Nothing." Eric's tone was sharp. "I'm just tired of being told I can't do what I want because it's different from what everyone else is doing. You guys can stay here and be the cows. I'm done with it."

Then, as Eric stormed off, Mike shouted after him, "You'd better start bulking up because your next fight is going to be with me."

With his back turned to us, my brother rose his middle finger in the air and Mike laughed. By grade twelve, Mike had developed an incredible amount of muscle mass but, in contrast to my brother's predisposition to fighting, Mike refrained.

Two months later, Eric vanished. He left without saying a word, not to my parents, not to Mike, and not to me. My brother and I had been inseparable since birth and throughout our teen years, right up until that moment when Eric left for the military without telling anyone.

Our Uncle Stephen, a military man himself, searched for him but, by the time he found Eric, my brother already belonged to the military. And so, while Mike was playing football for Waterloo University and majoring in mathematics, Eric was off fighting an endless battle in Afghanistan.

A year later, when my brother returned home

on leave, my grandfather praised him for having the courage to follow his own path.

$$\S$$

Pulling up to Sam's house, Adrian honks the horn a couple of times. Then, he slides his arm across the back of my seat. "You know what you need?"

I flash him a sideways glance. "Don't you dare say it."

"You need a new man."

"You said it."

Sam pokes his head through the passenger window. "Who needs a man?"

"This one."

"And you need a bigger car," I snap back as I leap over the centre console and into the back seat.

"Why? I'm one person."

"Two," Sam says sliding into his seat and offering his boyfriend a kiss.

"Three," I add squeezed into the back and feeling claustrophobic. "And, for your information, dating's for people who are looking for a relationship. I'm nowhere near ready to move on."

"No one's telling you to move on," Adrian says as we pull out of Sam's driveway. "Just see what else is out there. You know, sample the pond."

"Excuse me?" Sam gawks at him.

"What? I'm not telling her to have sex with anyone. Just mingle a little." He glances back at me through the rearview mirror. "Who knows, you might come to realize that what you have is worth holding onto."

I scoff. "I don't want to meet anyone."

"Doom and gloom, Issy. That's what you are."

I shoot him a disapproving glare, all the while admiring the soft curls on the back of his head.

I don't want to meet someone new. It's too hard. Meeting someone, getting to know them, the whole psychological analysis that follows, it's just too damn hard. Suddenly, you're the most insecure version of yourself.

"You do it to yourself. You know that, don't you?"

"What is that supposed to mean?"

Adrian's eyes are still on me. "It means that you go into a funk and you stay there."

"I do not."

"Yes, you do. And this introvert thing of yours, it's not healthy."

Well, maybe if Mike hadn't developed a sudden personality flaw, and my brother didn't feel the need to plunge everyone into his chaos, maybe then I wouldn't be so damn doom and gloom.

Sam takes hold of Adrian's hand. "Take it easy on her. Breaks-ups are hard."

"I know they are."

"And she's injured."

Once again, Adrian meets my disconcerted gaze through the mirror. "Well, it's settled then. You're going with me and Sam this weekend."

"What?" Sam glares at him.

"She needs it. Look at her."

"It's a romantic getaway for two."

I shut the spat down quickly telling them, "Thanks for the offer but I'm not going to just up and leave like I have nothing else going on."

"Like what?" Adrian calls me out on my bullshit, as per usual. "Besides sitting in your sad and dreary room with a notebook and pen or clacking away on your laptop?" His eyebrows raise in that sardonic way of his. "Am I wrong?"

He's not wrong. That's exactly what I'm planning to do.

Adrian laughs. "Issy, the hermit. Your twenty-three years old, for God's sake. Put on some make-up and get out there."

"Sorry to bore you with my Plain-Jane effect."

Adrian smirks at me.

"Why don't you go out there -" I start to say, but Sam cuts me off.

"You two are like an old married couple," he tells us. "And you're giving me a headache."

Adrian pulls his gaze away from mine to look at his boyfriend as though sparking an old argument.

Arriving at my parent's house, Adrian pulls into the driveway where three vehicles are already parked. My eyes instantly lock onto my brother's black pick-up truck. Eric's home.

Ahead, my father stands on the porch with his hands at his waist. The sleeves of his dress shirt are rolled up exposing the tattoos on his forearms. On the right arm, there is an old Norse cross while on the left, he bears the insignia of a Celtic crest inscribed with the letters *ESB*.

As we step out of the vehicle, Adrian leans into me and whispers, "Are you ready for this?"

I turn to him with a smirk. "Are you?"

He shakes his head. Adrian is admittedly terrified of my father. I find it amusing, although, to be fair to Adrian, my father can be intimidating.

On most days, David Bauer looks like a badass in a corporate suit. With the dark cropped hair, the thin beard, and the piercing blue eyes, he makes anyone think twice before approaching. And yet, despite his brutish appearance, my father can be a softy.

"Isabella." As I step onto the porch, my father wraps me into a tight embrace. "You should have called. I would have picked you up."

"I'm fine, dad." He releases me and I motion to Adrian saying, "It was on his way."

Adrian follows me closely into the house, clipping my heals with his sneakers as my father follows us inside.

When I was young, I was convinced that my father was a gangster. I'd watched him pummel a guy who had stolen from our garage. The man ran away with a bloody face and tears in his eyes. Another time, my father caught Eric fighting behind our high school. With a bout of overconfidence, my brother tried to take on a couple of jocks. He might have won the fight too, had our father not broken them up.

From the field, I watched my father's SUV come to an abrupt halt. Then, with his sleeves rolled up and his fists clenched, he marched towards us. When he began tossing kids off my brother, I knew it was time to leave. Eric was dragged into the back seat of the vehicle, and we drove home in silence.

Later that day, seated across from my father, I watched as he ate his dinner as though nothing had happened. Still wearing his white button-up dress shirt, he placed a napkin over his lap, held the knife and fork in his hands, and cut into his meat.

When my mother asked him how his day went, if there was anything new, he simply stated, "Nope. Nothing new."

My father's eyes never left his plate, and my brother never said a word. I almost laughed out loud. My father, the gangster, it was a ridiculous notion.

Chapter 2   January 1986

"Shit, shit, shit, shit, shit." Damn water's as cold as the iron pump. Doesn't help that the temperature's plummeted below zero.

Rubbing my hands together, I dunk them under the water pump again. Then, I shut my eyes and my mouth tight and slap some of that cold water on my face too. I rub my hands together fast, trying to shake off the sting. If I had a rock and a stick, you'd think I was trying to start a fire.

Brushing away the gray-white chalk dust from my clothes and hair, I go into the usual coughing fit. Finally, I throw on my jacket, pull my cap tight over my head, and set off across the London brickyard towards home.

Home is the town of Northampton. The area has been run down for years, but no one gives a crap. This place used to be a gem, or at least that's what I've heard from the old people that remember it that way. I only know it as home. This is the place where I grew up, went to school, and met my childhood friends. It's also the place where I won my first fight, had my first drink, lost my virginity; all my firsts happened here.

Twenty minutes later, I enter the front door of my father's home and instantly, I'm aware of the silence. Mum passed away one year ago, leaving us boys in the care of our father. It might not seem like such a tragic story if John Bauer wasn't a raging drunk.

In the hallway, I unzip my jacket while my gaze drifts across the living room and comes to rest on the yellow-stained mantle. This is the place where my father keeps the leather strap. It's laid here in plain view as a reminder of the punishment that awaits us should we ever disobey him. Except that now, aside from the cracks and the dust, the ledge lays empty.

My father is a man of little patience, eager to strike at the slightest revolt. Over the years, I endured my share of beatings. But now, nearing twenty years of age, I'd grown tall and strong, and the old man had grown reluctant.

This reluctance occurred in succession. As my brothers and I grew and began to defend ourselves, the old man began to back off. There was only one of us still young and timid.

Eddie had been born much later; an accident, no doubt, because how could any woman stand to go near a brute of a man like my father. Yet, as small and fragile as my mother seemed to me, she had handled my father well, and she'd kept the peace in the home for as long as she was alive.

A shrilling scream pierces the air and pulls my attention towards the back of the house. Across the living room, through the kitchen, and out the back door, I follow the wailing cries. Throwing the rotting shed door open, I find Eddie cowering in the corner while the old man lashes him with the whip. The boy had just turned thirteen years old.

The fearful look in my brother's eyes was unbearable; I couldn't stop myself from reacting. Lunging forward, I knock the old man down and, with little effort, pry the strap from his shaking hands. Then, I turn to the boy and tell him to lift his trousers.

"I'll kill you," my father hisses, struggling to rise to his feet. "You little bastard, I'll tear you apart."

The sudden stomping of boots draws my attention towards the side of the yard.

"What the hell's going on?" My brothers' run up behind me. Will, reaching me first, pulls me from the shed, while Richard takes hold of a tearful, red-faced Eddie and leads him away.

"Shit." Will grumbles under his breath and I follow my brother's gaze to the back of the shed. There, I see my father's aged and darkened figure creep towards the back corner of the room.

My father isn't a large man, however, he envelops a fury that when unleashed can rival the toughest of men. His own tale is a woeful one. It's a story of a father who was lost to the war and a widowed mother who'd struggled to feed and clothe her children.

John Bauer never spoke of his parents and, what little I knew of them, I had heard from my mother. She knew little of them herself, but she had once told me that the children were often left alone. John, at seven years of age, watched over his five-year-old sister while their mother went to work. She left at nightfall and returned to them in the early hours of the morning.

"David…" Will's voice breaks my thoughts, and I follow his bewildered gaze. From inside the shed, my father comes towards us, his hunting rifle clenched in his hands. "Run!"

Once again, I set off running. Across the row of townhomes and around the wooden fence, I keep running as fast as I can.

"You'd better run, boy." My father shouts from somewhere over the fence. "You ever come back here, I'll kill you with my bare hands."

My jacket undone and flapping in the crisp evening air, I move without pause. I run with that leather strap in my hand until it feels like a knife cutting into my skin. At last, I toss it into the swells of the river that carry it away.

Reaching the park, I drop onto a bench. With the bitter cold at my face and resentment filling my eyes, I remain there. As night falls, I make my way to a coffee shop.

Staring blankly into a stained ceramic mug, I tell myself that everything will be okay. I had saved up some money. I'd find a flat or rent a room. I'd be fine.

When exhaustion sets in, I lay my head on my forearms and shut my eyes. Just for a moment, I tell myself. It isn't until a hand rattles my shoulders that I come to.

"This isn't a hotel, chum. Move along."

Work that day was tough. Every brick felt heavier than the one before. When evening came, I found myself sitting at another coffee shop. But that night, I decided to return to the only place I could think to go.

Entering through the side door of the old brick factory, I creep towards the back of the warehouse where the supplies are kept, and no one seldom enters. There, over a pile of dismantled boxes, I lay down and close my eyes.

"Hey!" The loud rumble forces me awake and I look up to find a large man with thick eyebrows and a deep scowl looking down at me. "Get up."

I hurry to my feet. "I'm sorry -" I struggle to get the words out. "I just needed a place for the night."

The man reaches for me. "Wait." I slap his hand away and try to reason with him "You don't understand. It was a mistake."

"You're damn right it was."

He grabs me by the jacket and, again, I push him back. "I work here."

"Not anymore, you don't."

A security guard approaches. He's large and wide and he has tattoos creeping up the side of his neck. "You're coming with me," he says.

The security guard grabs me. I pull away. He reaches for me again and, this time, I strike him across the face. I don't know why I did it. It was the excitement, I suppose.

My mother would have said, as she often did, that the apple doesn't fall far from the tree. She didn't say it out of malice or regret; she understood me. Even as a child, when my temper was out of control or my attention span wavered, my mother knew what to do. Sometimes, she could smooth things over with as little as a mug of warm cocoa and some conversation. But, as I grew and the bad days worsened, the leather strap was often the result.

Even then, after my father left me, my mother would step into my room, brush away the tears, and tell me how sorry she was. When she embraced me, I could feel the dampness from her cheeks transfer onto mine. I didn't understand why she was sad; she wasn't the one who hurt me. Of course, I would eventually come to know the power of regret.

With both men now closing in on me, I do the only thing that I can – I run. In the dimmed morning light, I race back down Saxon Road. I keep running until I arrive at The Grounds Café.

I enter, breathless. A man with a bushy beard watches me from one of the tables. Collecting myself, I make my way to the counter and order a coffee and a donut. Then, taking a seat by the window, I shut my eyes and lower my head.

"You alright, son?"

Looking across the room at the bearded man, I

force a grin before returning my gaze to my coffee mug and plate of crumbs. I'm still hungry but mostly I'm exhausted, and I can feel my mind drifting into darkened places. All I want is sleep.

"Don't stress yourself too much." The man is still talking to me with his heavy accent. "You're young. Things will work out, they always do. And besides," he rises and places his cap onto a well-groomed head of hair. "You know what they say? When life gives you lemons..." Somewhere underneath the reddish-brown beard, there's a smile.

"Well, I'm off," he says.

As he turns to leave, I ask, "Is that your truck out there?"

He glances out the window. It's the only vehicle in the parking lot and he's the only other customer in the place. "Yup, that's my girl."

"Where you headed?"

"London. Where else?"

Jake at work used to say, "All roads lead to London." He left weeks ago, heading out there for a better life. I envied him.

The large man now tips his cap to me saying, "Best of luck to you, son," and turns away.

Sitting there alone in the café, I watch him as he heads out the door. When the truck's engine starts up, I inch forward in my seat and, when the truck begins to move, desperation sets in.

"No, wait." I jump to my feet and hurry out the door. Waving my arms frantically, I run in front of the headlights yelling, "Stop."

The truck's breaks squeal to a halt. Climbing onto the truck, I pull the passenger door open.

"What the hell is the matter with you?" The man's voice pierces my eardrums. "Are you trying to get yourself killed, huh? And me in jail for murder?"

"I'm sorry. It's my mother." I didn't know what else to say. "She's not well. I need to get to London to see her." Sitting in that shop feeling utterly alone, she was all I could think of.

The expression on the man's face softens. "Ah..." he grumbles at me. "Get in."

I jump in and shut the door. Leaning against the large bucket seat, I exhale and let my shoulders fall.

"I'm Red, by the way. That's what people call me." We turn onto the main road. "You'd think it's because of the beard, but it's not. It's 'cause my face gets bright red when I drink. That's how you can tell I've been drinking." He laughs. It's a loud, hearty sound that fills the truck.

"So," Red glances over at me. "Mind if I ask what happened to your mam?"

Cancer. Two years ago, my mother was diagnosed with cancer. First, it was in her stomach. Then it spread into her intestines. Eventually, it was everywhere.

"I'm sorry to hear it."

We veer onto the M1 and I turn to the side-view mirror as the distance between me and home expands. This is another first.

"Has she been in the hospital long, your mam?"

I nod. I wish. If only I could talk to her, ask her what I should do.

"She's going to pull through," Red tells me.

I explain that she won't, but he insists. "She has to. For your sake, son, she has to."

I force a grin and thank him for saying that, wishing so much that it was true.

Red and I part on the outskirts of Brixton. From there, I find a dark underground pub that smells distinctly of alcohol and vomit. With a double shot of Irish Whiskey in me, I plot my next steps.

Three double shot's later, I overhear two men discussing a package delivery gone wrong. Seated further down the bar, their drunken whispers carry. The package was to be delivered across town that night but, their "pansy" went AWOL. They couldn't do it themselves, was my understanding. It had to be delivered by someone unknown.

"I'll do it." The words fly out of my mouth without thought.

The men, both with similar buzzed haircuts and messy beards, turn to me.

"What did you say?"

"I said, I'll do it."

They laugh, and I turn in my seat to face them. Three days into my nomadic existence, a patchy beard now covers my face. It looks like I've tried to carve a bad design onto my chin, like those crop circles that no one can figure out. Worse than that, my hair is a greasy mess, not unlike the beard, and I don't smell too good. But, despite my lack of facial hair and hygiene, I'm not a kid anymore and I'll take whatever they throw at me.

"I said, I'll deliver your package," I repeat with more confidence. "For the right price."

I didn't bother to ask what was in the cardboard box, nor who I was delivering it to. None of that mattered. What mattered was that at the end of the delivery, I would find myself a modest motel, take the longest, hottest shower of my life, eat a warm meal in front of a television set, and sleep like an insomniac after a two-month stint of sleep deprivation. It was going to be great.

I arrive at the address in Uxbridge late into the night and drop the package off at the front door of a tall home. Once the job's complete, I return to Brixton.

The second address provided to me is located at a large warehouse. I was to go around to the back door and knock three times. When the rusty door opens, I find myself face-to-face with a large hairy man.

"Who the hell are you?" he asks.

"I was told to come here after the delivery," I explain. "To see Mr. Barton."

The scowl on the man's protruding forehead subsides. "Come in."

I follow him through a long dark hallway, and down a set of metal steps leading into an open space. A boxing ring occupies the centre of the warehouse. Along the back wall, an insignia reads, 'The East Side Boys Fight Club'.

"This way," the man barks at me.

We turn down another hallway. This one is lit up bright. Halting in front of a metal door, the man knocks, and the thick voice on the other side tells us to enter.

Behind a desk sits a man with wide shoulders and a long face. He wears a dark suit jacket over a white dress shirt with the top buttons undone. When he looks up at us, his blue eyes twinkle under the florescent lighting.

"Speak." The oaf shoves me forward. I glare back at him and the man's brow deepens.

I slow my breaths and focus instead on the man behind the desk. "Hello. I'm David. I delivered the package to Uxbridge today."

The man leans back in his chair. "Did anyone see you?" he asks, smoothing over the thinning hair on his head.

"No, sir."

"Did you see anyone?"

I'd walked along the street observing the flow of traffic and pedestrians. It was a quiet neighbourhood, hence, limited witnesses.

"There was no one around when I dropped off the package," I tell him.

"You're certain?"

"Yes, sir. I'm sure." This time, I speak without hesitation, and the man smiles.

"Well, then. It seems we have ourselves our new delivery boy."

Chapter 3   August 2016

"I'm fine." Standing in our living room, I pull my bandaged arm from my grandmother's grasp and wave my mother's hand away from my face. All the while, my grandfather's commenting on our crumbling society.

"It was an accident," I tell them. "Everything's okay."

I flash Adrian a disgruntled look. He warned me to call ahead and inform my family of the ordeal. "It'll give them time to absorb the news and let it sink in," he said. Good thing I listened because this is the aftermath of that conversation.

"Who did it?" Stephen asks, standing alongside his young wife, Emily, and their two-year-old daughter.

"I don't know," I say.

Eric emerges from the kitchen. Standing shoulder

to shoulder with Stephen, my brother watches me. A frown forms over his face as Adrian explains that the police are investigating the incident.

Years ago, my brother would have proclaimed society's flaws or my lack of awareness towards my surroundings. His thoughts have since changed, receding along with the chaos in his mind.

The conversation carries on into the dining room. Everyone is speaking all at once, but it's my grandfather's voice that is heard above everyone else's. "What is this world coming to?"

"Chaos," someone murmurs. "Utter chaos."

Emily holds onto her daughter a little tighter, and my mother flashes me a sweet and sympathetic smile.

She worries, I know that, but I'm fine. Then, as my grandfather starts up on the recent attacks on London and Paris, the room erupts into loud chatter. Everyone has something to say, except for Stephen and Eric. They nod now and then, glance at one another from time to time, but otherwise remain silent participants.

They both served in Afghanistan and they both made it home. "Unlike so many others," they'll often remind us. When they look to one another in that silent way of theirs, I realize that there is an unspoken language between them, a well-kept secret that only they are privy to.

"And now there's another one brewing," my grandfather says. "And who knows how this one's going to turn out."

"God only knows," my mother remarks.

My father smiles across at her. "Sara, love, why

don't you have a seat so we can get started."

"Well…" My grandfather pours himself another glass of wine. "Like I always told my boy, when death's staring you square in the face, you know it's your time to get the hell out or join the parade."

My father looks across at Stephen. "Good words to live by, I suppose."

Stephen laughs.

"I think we're in for something brand new here," my grandfather continues. "Something the world has never seen."

"I'm afraid you might be right about that, dad." Stephen has something to say, after all.

Seated at the other end of the dining room table, Stephen holds his young daughter over his lap with one arm. The sleeve of his other arm is pinned up at the elbow.

"Stop it. All of you." My grandmother has heard enough. She can't stand it when they start-up like this. "This is all we ever talk about," she cries out. "War, war, and more war! Have we not had enough of it?" Standing by her chair, her dark hair up in a tight ponytail, she looks to her son. "There's nothing brewing or stirring or scalding for that matter. Just leave it alone. Talk about something else, for goodness sake."

My grandmother, the spokesperson for humanity.

Stephen looks across at Eric and my brother raises his eyebrows in response. Stephen is twelve years our senior. He joined the Royal Canadian Army Cadets at fourteen years of age, enlisted in the Armed Forces at seventeen, then climbed up the ranks to Captain.

Even after he lost his arm in action in '09, he retained a desk job until his retirement from the forces last year. However, what ate away at him wasn't the missing arm at all.

When Stephen returned from his final tour in Kabul, we expected that he would return to us the same way as when he'd left. In our minds, the months he had spent away were nothing more than a minor ripple in time, as though time itself had stood still for him while our lives carried on. But, when Stephen walked through our front door with the empty sleeve and the darkness in his eyes, it was evident that my uncle would never be the same.

"I lost it when my guys lost their lives," he had told us. "Guess I got the better deal, didn't I?"

It was a twisted joke. The day that Stephen lost the arm, he also lost four of his troops to an IED, an improvised explosive device. The bomb was buried under the desert sands. It tore their vehicle to pieces. Stephen later admitted that he would have rather died out there with his men than come home with this constant reminder.

Yet, much has changed for my uncle since his return. Stephen's wife and daughter afforded him a fresh start and, although the guilt remains, Stephen learned to accept his survival.

While a new debate breaks out over something lighter, food, I look across the table at my brother. I'm thrilled to see the darkness faded from his eyes and the anger erased from his face; the old Eric has resurfaced. Of course, he's still incognito with his signature black t-shirt and dark loose-fitted jeans.

"How long are you home this time?" I ask.

He leans in the chair and slides his arm across his fiancé's shoulders. "The whole long weekend," he says.

Victoria smiles at him. "And this time, I'm forcing him to stay the full three days." Eric groans and Victoria pokes his belly. "You promised."

"I know."

Eric and Victoria dated briefly before my brother left for the military. When he returned, they rekindled and, during the Christmas holidays Eric proposed. There remained great debates on the wedding date, but they assured us that it would be settled soon enough.

"By the way," Eric changes the subject. "Matt's coming down too."

"He is?" My smile is instant. "When?"

"Tonight, I think."

Matt Hamilton, the greatest person on earth. If it wasn't for Matt, I don't know what would have happened to my brother.

"How is everything going at the Centre, anyway?" I ask.

"Great." Eric and Victoria look to one another. "It's not at all what I expected, and everything I could ever want."

My brother had become employed at the Hamilton-West Centre in Ottawa where he had carried out his therapy. Now, he was helping other military veterans get back on their feet.

Looking at my twin with admiration, I tell him, "I'm really happy for you."

Eric dismisses the remark. He's never fully accepting of praise. "How about you?" he asks. "How've things been with you?"

I lower my eyes to my plate. "Fine," and catch Adrian shaking his head in response. "I'm fine," I insist with a light tap at his thigh.

"When was the last time you spoke to him?" Eric asks.

"I don't want to talk about this." He knows that.

"Issy." Eric speaks in his 'I'm serious' tone. "Talk to him."

"Why?"

"Because he wants to talk to you."

"I have nothing to say."

"Issy..."

"Stop."

His eyes focus onto mine. "Put yourself in Mike's shoes."

"Peanut butter and Jelly, that's what you said."

My brother chuckles to himself. "I know."

§

The last time that Mike and I spoke was the same day that we fell apart. I had been staying at his place since graduation. We talked about moving in together and, although we had our ups and downs, it felt like the right time to take the next step. So, four months ago, I moved half of my closet into Mike's apartment. I bought an extra toothbrush, hairbrush, and facewash, all for the sake of staying with Mike. We were certain that we'd be together forever. It took one single event for it all to come crumbling down, like a lopsided human pyramid.

One evening, Mike came home to find Adrian lying in bed with me. I was bundled underneath the comforter, sniffling and coughing. My eyes were swollen, and my nose felt like it was on fire from all the tissue wiping. Adrian lay over the comforter, fully clothed, feeding me chicken noodle soup that he'd picked up on his way over.

We met five months before in the elevator of the building after Adrian purchased a condo unit on the top floor. We hit it off instantly.

"It's unnatural the way he acts with you," Mike fumed after Adrian left the apartment. "It's like he's trying to rub it in my face."

"Rub what?" I tossed the used tissue at him. "What is he rubbing in your face, Mike?"

Mike didn't answer.

Adrian and I had grown increasingly casual with one another. It drove Mike nuts. But there was nothing malicious or deceptive in our relationship. We were just great friends.

"If Mia or Taylor were here, you wouldn't say anything."

"Your girlfriends aren't trying to hit on you."

I glowered at him. "You don't like him because you've chosen not to like him."

"I don't like him because of how much he likes you."

Heated by the argument and my raging fever, I threw back the covers, jumped out of bed, and moved towards him. "Well, right now, I like him a whole lot more than I like you."

Mike grabbed his keys and stormed out of the apartment shouting, "I'm done with this."

Soon after, I also left the apartment - with all my belongings. Returning to my parent's house, I dropped my suitcase on the floor and called Eric.

"Your friend's an idiot," I yelled through the phone. After I'd calmed down, I told my brother what transpired.

Eric thought nothing of my relationship with Adrian. "It's as natural as peanut butter and jelly," he'd said. Nor did my brother understand Mike's distaste for the guy, which left Mike feeling insulted. Mike presumed that his best friend, of all people, would advocate for him. But Eric, aside from referencing peanut butter and jelly once again, didn't feel that there was anything amiss.

Who knew that my wayward brother would become the voice of reason?

§

"He's going to want to talk to you when he gets here," Eric now tells me.

"You invited him?"

"Of course."

I look at him in awe. "Why would you do that?"

He lifts one shoulder. "He's my friend. And I haven't seen him in months."

"You haven't seen any of us in months."

Eric smirks. I don't know if he's trying to play

matchmaker, or just trying to get a rise out of me. Either way, he's pissing me off.

"You're unbelievable," I tell him.

"And you need to get your shit together."

"You, of all people, are going to lecture me about getting my shit together?" The remark overwhelms me with insurmountable anger. "You, who couldn't see straight for a year?"

Eric's face falls.

§

One year ago, nearly to the day, my brother met Matt during a drunken frenzy at a local pub. Eric was yelling at the bartender because Brian refused to serve him another shot. After his return from Afghanistan, Eric struggled. "This is the only way I'll get any sleep," he'd say.

Brian had a soft spot for my brother. Maybe because he could still remember the little runt from high school who'd gone off and done the unthinkable, done what the rest of us could never do. But that day, my brother was out of control. Eric became violent.

Reaching across the bar, he took hold of Brian by the collar. When Matt tried to intervene, Eric swung at him and missed.

"That's it." Brian had enough. He picked up the phone but Matt, always the peacekeeper, stopped him saying, "It's alright. I got this."

"Fuck off." Eric was slurring terribly. "You ain't got shit."

But my brother's bad behaviour didn't deter Matt. "Look, man, I just want to help you."

"You want to help me?" Eric lost his mind. "You think I'm some kind of charity case, is that it? Get the hell away from me before I knock you on your ass. You know, on account of my post-war issues."

"Go ahead." Matt had been through this so many times that nothing fazed him anymore. "If it'll make you feel better, go ahead."

So, Eric swung his fist and, this time, he didn't miss. Afterwards, Matt drove my brother home. When they arrived, I thanked him for returning Eric and apologized for the bloody lip.

"It's not a problem," Matt told me. "I deal with this sort of thing all the time."

"Drunks," I remarked.

"No," Matt corrected me. "War vets."

I felt like an ass, and I never again made assumptions where the military was concerned. Then, Matt offered Eric a once-in-a-lifetime opportunity, a chance to clean himself up and get back on his feet again. It's amazing to me how one person can have such an impact on a life.

§

However, in his pursuit to not "follow the herd," my brother put us all through hell. For the last four years, we have been consumed by worry. From the moment that my brother left until three months ago when Matt gave him the "green light," a sort of graduation from the Centre, we worried. As a result, my parents grew tired and distant, my grandparents became anxious, continuously checking up on us, while Stephen became guilt-ridden. He felt somehow responsible for Eric.

And me? I fell apart and, by the time I'd caught my breath, I couldn't comprehend who I'd become. Even now that my brother had healed and was moving on, I still hadn't climbed out of this rut. I'd lost everything: my job, an entire semester of school, Mike.

Despite all of this, I regret my words. Until Eric leans across the table and says, "Kind of like your relationship with Mike, huh? Shitty and all over the place."

I'm stunned by the remark and it takes me a moment to collect my thoughts. But, once I do, my words spill out in one breath, without pause, or reflection.

"My relationship might have been shitty and filled with all sorts of gaping holes, but that's on you. If I didn't have to worry about finding you pissed drunk and passed out in the backyard, or half-baked somewhere then, maybe, my relationship with Mike might not have been so damn strained and so fucking difficult."

This is what it boiled down to; I had become my brother's keeper, the keeper of all things Eric.

Eric's arms fall at his sides, and the fire in his eyes fades away. "You're right," he says. "That one's on me."

Without another word, I hurry away from the table.

"Issy." My grandfather calls out to me. "Grab another bottle of wine from the fridge."

The kitchen door swings shut behind me. With my hands to my face, I lean against the cold granite counter and allow the tears to rush in. I shouldn't have said what

I said. It isn't my brother's fault that things worked out the way they did. Eric went out there intending to make a difference. That was his reason for joining the army, and it was an admirable reason. But fate had other plans for him. That's how my mother justified all the horrible things in life; it was fate.

Chapter 4   June 1988

Driving along King's Avenue, I catch sight of a brawl in mid-session. In an unlit alleyway, a large man faces three others.

"Come on," he shouts. He has a thick Irish accent and his fists are held at eye-level. "I'll take the lot of 'ya."

Intrigued, I pull over on the other side of the road. All four men are stumbling over themselves and slurring but, the big guy, he's throwing punches like he knows what he's doing. He hits one man in the face, and the guy goes down. He strikes the second man square in the jaw, and he also falls. I turn off the ignition and step out of the vehicle just as the third guy runs away.

Snickering at the scene, I make my way across the

road. "Hey, Irish."

Considering his drunken state, the speed at which he turns to me with his fists blazing is unexpected. But that's when I realize that he's not so much a man, as he is a kid. He can't be more than nineteen years old.

With my hands in the air, I ask, "Are you a boxer?"

"Aye – you don't see m' fists?"

I can't help but laugh. The kids got spunk. "Take it easy, mate. I'm not here to fight you. I want to offer you a job."

"A job?" The kid's fists drop to his sides, and I introduce myself with an outstretched hand.

"Patrick," he says. "Patrick O'Reilly." It takes him another minute to shake my hand. Not the trusting type - good on him.

"How would you like to fight for me, Patrick O'Reilly?"

"Am I gettin' paid?"

I smile - easiest job in the world. "Yeah, you're getting paid."

"Hm," Patrick ponders the idea. "Well, it is m' birthday."

It was an easy gig. All Patrick had to do was remain standing for three rounds. The kid was a natural; Patrick couldn't be beat. Men tried. They fought with all their might, but they couldn't beat the "Lucky Irish" as he came to be known. And the money was great, for Patrick and for me.

I'd never had it so good. Two years ago, I didn't have a bed to sleep in. Now, I had the bed, the sofa, and the whole damn apartment to myself, even if it was only temporary because everything has an end. My father instilled that notion into us long ago. My youth, my mother, my life as I knew it, it all had an end.

"And don't you forget it," my father would say. "No matter how good you think you are, or how tough, or how smart, it all has an end. Just like your mother. She had beauty and brains, but she couldn't escape her illness. It came and took her away, so you make sure you take what you can while you can."

That's what I had learned from my father. And so, the day that Patrick fell, as difficult as it was to watch, it didn't come as a great surprise.

Patrick was struck in the head. His opponent wasn't a big guy, but he was fast and the hit came out of nowhere. Patrick crumbled into a heap in the centre of the ring while I watched from the sidelines. He went on to win the fight that night, but the hit had left him disoriented and there was a terrible ringing in his ears.

"The kid doesn't look right," I tell Barton. "We should postpone the next fight."

From behind his metal desk, Barton scoffs, "The kid's fightin' and that's that. I don't want to hear another word about it."

The next evening, I'm once again at ringside. Patrick strikes his opponent dead-on. The guy falls, and the crowd cheers. Patrick turns to me with a smirk. The fight had just begun, and Patrick's back to his usual antics. Then, from the corner of my eye, I catch a glimpse of the other boxer. He's up on his feet and moving fast across the ring.

"Patrick." I call out to him, but it's too late.

With a tremendous blow, the boxer strikes Patrick across the side of the head. He teeters from side to side and falls. This time, Patrick doesn't rise.

Eight months after it had begun, it was over.

"What the hell was that?" Barton belts out in the change room as Patrick heaves into the toilet. "You cost me thousands tonight, you piece of shit."

Standing between Patrick and Barton, I snap back at the brute of a man. "I told you he wasn't ready."

"You, shut up."

"You pay me to manage the fights. How the hell can I do my job when you keep taking that authority away from me?"

Barton's rage turns on me. "I pay you to win fights not lose them." He points a rigid finger to the back of Patrick's head. "You're through, Irish, you hear me? Through."

Barton then looks to the large man at his side. His name is Jack Devons, Barton's top henchman. "Grab him," Barton instructs. "Let's get this over with."

In this dirty business, loyalty is your only saviour. A man is either loyal to the boss and therefore useful, or he becomes useless and thereby disloyal. This is how Idris Barton governs his business and his men. Hence, once a man is no longer useful, he is deemed disloyal and so, he becomes untrustworthy. Barton can't simply allow untrustworthy men to walk free. There's too much at stake. The only way to handle these types of men is to be rid of them, and Barton deals with them the only way he knows how.

As Barton's thug comes forward, I block his path. "What the hell do you think you're doing, Bauer?" Devons snarls.

"I can't let you do this."

The man tries once more to get past me and I knock him down.

"You piece of shit." Barton storms towards me.

I strike the man twice across the face and he hits the ground. "Run," I tell Patrick, now standing at my side. "Go, damn it."

Patrick flees.

"Have you gone mad?" Barton and his goon rise.

I'd grown a soft spot for the kid. I felt responsible for him, and there was no way that Patrick could have withstood another blow to the head. It would have killed him. That was the intent, of course. I couldn't stand by and do nothing.

I'd been gagged, tossed into the back of a car trunk, and hauled out to Barton's country estate. Lying on the cold concrete floor of the basement, my eyes swollen half shut, I roll onto my back with a grunt. Every inch of my body aches.

"You're not so tough, are you?" Devons hovers over me. His knuckles are bloodied, and his forehead glistens. "The only reason you're not dead is because Barton wants to do it himself." He grabs me by the hair and leans in so close that I can smell the booze and cigarette smoke on his breath. "And when we're done with you," he sneers, "we're going to find your friend. And you can't imagine the things we're gonna do to him."

"Better than sucking off the old man's -" My head hits the concrete.

When I come to, there's a red-bearded giant standing over me.

"You remember, Titan, don't you?" Devons voice echoes.

How can I forget? The man stands at six feet, five inches and his arms are the size of my thighs.

"Feeling scared?" The large ape smiles down at me. "'Cause you should be." With little effort, he flips me onto my stomach.

"Hold him still," Devons says, "I wanna get this right."

With my face pressed to the concrete, I feel something hot singe the back of my neck. It stings like hell and I fight to free myself.

"Steady him," Devons barks.

I can smell the char of burning flesh but, it's the surge of excruciating pain that causes me to struggle harder. Titan's grip intensifies. He pushes down on my head until I feel like my skull is going to cave in, and I let out a scream.

Finally, I'm released, but I don't move. I just lay there with my head spinning and my body throbbing.

Much later that day, I awaken with the creak of the basement door. It's daylight again. As the footsteps descend, I force myself to sit up. Groaning, I place a hand to the delicate spot on my ribs.

"Ah, good, you're up."

I look across the room. Devons' brought reinforcements. I recognize Khan. We'd worked together on occasion, but I've never seen the kid that's standing next to him. With that lanky body and barely a stubble on his chin, he's much too young to be involved in this shit.

"I think he's pissed himself," Titan laughs.

"Ah, come on." Devons turns to the kid. "Eddie, give him the food. Then, go get him a bucket or something."

The kid sets the plate down in front of me and hands me a bottle of water. I gulp it down greedily.

"Hey." He leans in closer. "Slow down, will 'ya. This is all you get."

"What the hell are you saying to him?" Devons kicks the kid in the ass. "Go on." The kid turns and leaves. "You, get up," Devons says to me, but I don't make a move. "I said get up." He pulls a gun on me and presses it to my forehead.

With effort, I rise to my feet.

"Now, you're going to tell me what I want to know, or you won't make it until Barton gets here, do you understand me?"

I stare the man in the face. "You know what you are? You're a fuckin' puppet," I hiss. "You've got Barton's fist so far up your ass -" Devons' pistol sweeps across my face and cuts my cheek.

I can't contain the anger that boils inside of me. In an explosive rage, I hit Devons across the face, and he drops the gun. A fearsome commotion breaks out as I leap for the weapon.

"Get the gun," Devons bellows. "Get the bloody gun."

The cold metal is at my fingertips when a boot strikes me across the cheek tearing the cut wide open. The blow forces me back. Without warning, they jump on me and, for the next thirty minutes, they beat me while the kid stands back watching.

I tried to fight back. I tried to defend myself, but it was useless. It wasn't until my eyes rolled up into my head, and my body went limp that they left me. For a long while afterward, I lay on the floor, spitting up blood and struggling to stay awake. I was sure that this was how my life would end, at twenty-three, in a gangster's basement, surrounded by my own blood and urine.

For four days and three nights, I endured this hell. Each morning I was awakened with a cigarette to the back of the neck, followed by water and scraps. This was how I came to measure my days. Then, in the evenings, after the sun went down and the basement darkened, I was again beaten to the brink of delirium and, it was in those beatings, that I again lost my sense of time.

In the end, Patrick came to my rescue, along with a couple of guys who'd grown loyal to me. And this time, we shot our way out.

I wish I hadn't said what I said...

Wrapping my arms around myself, I turn towards the French doors and look out to the backyard. This is the place where my brother and I played as children, running about the Bauer Castle with our bedsheet capes floating behind us and our toilet roll swords piercing the air. We had chased after imaginary dragons in the shapes of small birds and explored the safari that was our backyard. We'd feasted on worms and snails at dinner, which my mother insisted was just pasta and meatballs. Eric and I laughed because secretly, we knew the truth.

Unlocking the doors, I step onto the deck. Just ahead

of the patio stairs, the cobblestone pathway slithers along the grass and coils around the small pond where two iron benches face one another. There's a couple of fish in that pond and, sometimes, a tiny frog comes to visit. Further out, the old wooden fence dividing our yard from the forest looks worse than I remember. It's cracked in places and broken in others. This is why the deer keep coming into our yard. I'd told my parents a dozen times. Why don't they listen?

I raise my hands to my face and allow the tears to spill. I'd warned them about Eric too, before things got out of control. I know how much he suffered after his return from Afghanistan, how much he'd struggled to reach a new level of normality. I was there by his side through much of it, and I too suffered with him. First, at the abandoned field where Eric tried to take his life and again in Ottawa, at the Hamilton-West Centre in Room B, where my brother tried to convince us that his life wasn't worth living.

§

In November of 2013, Eric received an honourable medical discharge, but we wouldn't get word of it for close to four months. During those months, my brother didn't call, he didn't write; we imagined the worst. Once again, it was Stephen who went digging for information and the news was devastating. Eric had been hurt.

A missile strike, intended for Eric's unit, hit a building resulting in numerous civilian casualties. A heavy artillery battle ensued with the enemy. Eric was injured and, soon after, my brother was discharged from duty due to what Stephen called "mental incapacitation." It was all he said, either because it was all he knew, or he didn't want to say anymore.

Months later, seated on one of those cold iron benches in our yard with the breeze at my back and my hands tucked into my jacket, I thought of my brother. I sat there often during those days, wondering and worrying, when something caught my attention. From the corner of the house, a tall and lean figure appeared. Wearing military khakis and a black tuque, a man crossed the yard. I watched his long, methodical strides as he approached. The dark, shallow eyes that looked back at me were weathered, and his cheeks were sunken under a dense beard. My heart sank. Eric had returned to us, but the set of deep grey eyes were no longer those of the boy I once knew. My brother was different; he seemed lost.

Feeling that he no longer had direction or purpose, Eric bought himself an old, rusted pickup truck and headed into the country. He didn't have to venture far. Two kilometres up the lakeshore, he found an abandoned field with a run-down barn.

Lying in the back of the truck, staring up into the evening sky, Eric drank his worries away. On a couple of occasions, Mike and I went out there with him. It seemed harmless. We gazed up at the stars, drank beer, and chatted about life.

One time, Eric was feeling especially philosophical, describing the placement of the stars and the names of the constellations. This, somehow, led to the meaning of life. My brother had some strange ideas on that account, talking about human pawns in a chess game played by invisible aliens.

Mike teased him saying, "Man, you've changed, my friend."

"How so?" my brother asked.

"You used to be bold and fearless. And now, you hide away in abandoned fields conspiring about alien puppeteers."

Eric snickered. "Better than having to explain to people why I've changed so much."

"Touché." Mike tapped Eric's beer with his. Then, with sudden reverence, he said, "I still can't believe you're back. Almost three years." He shook his head. "That's a long time, dude."

Eric remained silent.

"When you went missing all those months..." Mike turned his face towards my brother's and leaned in close. "I thought that I might never see you again."

Eric, with a sly grimace, uttered, "You're not going to kiss me, are you?"

Mike shoved him. "You ass."

Eric laughed out loud while the beer foamed out of his bottle.

It had been a long time since I'd heard my brother laugh like that.

But Eric had good days and bad days, both masked by pills and alcohol. I didn't understand it at the time; I didn't know what was going on in my brother's head.

One night, late in January, I came home to find my

brother passed out on one of the deck chairs; empty beer bottles lay scattered around him. His lips had turned blue, and I struggled to wake him.

I managed to drag him into the house and get him on the sofa. I removed his sneakers and socks, forced dry, warm socks onto his feet, and covered him with a couple of blankets. The next morning, Eric got a good scolding.

"Okay, mom," he teased.

It infuriated me but, right after he said it, Eric lowered his gaze and uttered, "Don't tell mom and dad."

I agreed, but that was my mistake because the drunken episodes continued, and the fights escalated. At one point, my brother landed himself in the hospital after a nasty bar fight. Another time, Eric almost lost his license after he was caught with open alcohol in the front seat of his truck. On every occasion, I was there to bail him out, and I continued to keep his secrets.

Mike accused me of becoming so obsessed with rescuing my brother that, in the process, I had lost myself. Maybe, he was right. Maybe, I had become so wrapped up in my brother's life that I'd stopped living my own. Perhaps, my outburst at dinner that evening was out of resentment, but that couldn't be it. My love for my twin was unconditional or maybe there are conditions for every type of love.

§

The patio door opens. I turn around, my eyes barely dry, to find Mike standing there.

"Issy..." The gentle blue eyes lower to my bandaged arm before meeting my gaze once again. "Are you alright?"

I swallow the lump in my throat and try to calm my racing heart. "Yes. I'm fine. It was an accident."

He reaches for my arm, and I pull away again telling him that I'm fine.

"How are you fine?" His six-foot, two-inch square frame hovers over me. "This is not fine."

"Why are you here?" The harsh tone of my voice causes his eyebrows to gather. "I hope you're not going to start anything with Adrian."

"Of course, not."

Mike leans in closer, and I turn away. "Issy..." I can smell the sweetness of his cologne. "We should talk."

"There's nothing to talk about."

"It's been three weeks."

"Four," I correct him. "And like I said..." I turn to face him once again. "There's nothing to talk about."

Mike presses his lips together so that the dimples appear on his cheeks. "Look, we both said things that we didn't mean. We were angry."

"No, you said things. You were angry."

Mike opens his mouth to retaliate but instead he lets out an exasperated huff. Mike's a lot like a pressure cooker that needs to release steam before it blows its lid. Of course, in Mike's case, it would be his head – pop, right off.

The problem is that we're both too proud to admit the truth. Mike puts on a brave face rather than admit that he's wrong, and I'm just as bad. Here I am, standing in front of him and pretending like it isn't killing me when I know damn well that all I want is to throw my arms around him and never let go. But what bothers me most is how easy it was for him to give up on us. After everything we had been through together; I felt betrayed.

"I'm going back in," I tell him and, as I turn to leave, Mike takes hold of my good arm.

"You need to get over this thing," he says. "Or you're never going to move forward. We'll never move forward."

Forcibly, I pull away and go into the house. Entering the living room, my grandfather calls out, "Isabella, you forgot the wine."

I halt. Right, the damn wine. Turning around, I find Mike standing behind me with the bottle in his hand. Fighting against tears, I take the wine from him, set it onto the table, and hurry out the front door. We used to be so in sync. "Like a couple of peas in a pod," my mother would say. So, why had everything gone wrong?

"Why do you let him get to you like that?"

I'm back in Adrian's car. Slumped into the passenger's seat, I turn my face towards the window. But Adrian isn't referring to Mike right now. He's talking about Eric, the reason why I lose sleep, why I can't have a normal relationship, why I wake in the middle of the night in cold sweats.

"Don't worry," Adrian says. "Everything will work itself out. Tonight, you're going to live in the moment and force everything else out of your mind."

"That's right," Sam adds. "Trust in fate."

"There is no such thing," Adrian tells him.

"Why not?"

"Because coincidences don't exist. It's all a result of cause and effect. Your actions cause reactions."

As I think through Adrian's theory, I see my father step onto the front porch and I huff in an exhale of annoyance. "Can we get out of here?"

Chapter 6   March 1989

Stepping outside of Pearson Airport, Patrick gapes at the three feet of snow that surrounds us and gathers his jacket to his chest. "Where the hell did you bring us?"

His expression is priceless. No doubt, so is mine. I've never seen snow like this.

We settle into a two-bedroom apartment in a suburb known as Port Credit where the balcony overlooks Lake Ontario. The nice lady that showed us the apartment was extremely pleased with this feature. That's what she called it, a feature. I have to admit that it is a beautiful sight, if you can get past the stench that sweeps across the lake now and again.

The next task was to find a job. Although, money

wasn't as much of an immediate problem as it was explaining how we'd come about it. Transferring twenty thousand dollars into a Canadian bank account, questions were asked, and insinuations made.

"I owned a business back home," I tell the skinny woman seated on the other end of the desk.

"What sort of business?" she asks.

"Loans. Private lending."

"And you say you have no proof of this business?"

"Nope. All lost in the fire." Leaning against the chair, I unbutton my suit jacket to reveal my new dress shirt, fully aware of how the shirt hugs the curves of muscle on my chest and ribs.

The woman shifts in her seat. "Well…" Lowering her eyes from mine, she sweeps a strand of hair behind her ear. "I'm sure it won't be a problem. I'll just add a note here to state that it was an inheritance. That should cover any additional questions."

I smile at her and watch as her cheeks turn crimson red.

Three weeks later, the snow thawed, the trees bloomed, and Patrick found himself a job with a landscaping company.

"This is gonna change things," he says, his mildly freckled face brimming with excitement. "No more getting knocked in the face every day. It's like a dream come true," he jokes.

I'm happy for him because despite all of my misgivings and misjudgments, I was certain about one thing, Patrick couldn't afford another blow to the head.

Then, I too found a job, but I couldn't share Patrick's enthusiasm. The gig was a door-to-door sales job selling charity to unsuspecting housewives and retirees. The pitch was terrible, and the wages were even worse. I did it because I had to and, while I struggled to get through each day on the job, Patrick thrived. He enjoyed the work and the outdoors, but he was especially keen on the people.

Two months in, Patrick went to work at a home situated along the lakeshore.

"These people have their own private beach," he tells me. "It's incredible."

I sneer at the thought. Rich people don't appreciate what they have. They only know that they have it.

"And there's a girl," he adds with a ridiculous love-sick look on his face. "She's the most beautiful girl you've ever seen."

I beg to differ, but Patrick insists. He describes the Shermans' daughter as a young woman with long dark hair, a small rounded face with a slight swooping nose, a pair of big brown eyes, and a set of plump pink lips.

"She told me that I have the kindest eyes," he says smoothing his hand over his strawberry-blonde hair. "And she thinks I have a neat accent too. Neat, that's her word, not mine."

"I'm sure it's not your accent that she's interested in."

His smile widens. Women became giddy around Patrick, commenting on his blue-green eyes "with the hint of grey." But it was when Patrick flashed them that dimpled smile of his, followed by a humbled, "Hello, m' lady," that they swooned.

Popping the caps off a couple of beers, I hand Patrick a bottle and we head out onto the balcony.

He leans against the railing with a sulk. "But what the hell would she want with me, an ex-boxer that plays in the dirt?"

I raise my eyebrows to him. "You'd be surprised."

The sulk lifts from his face. "So, you think she'd go for me?"

"No."

"Why not?"

I take a seat in one of the fold-out chairs. "You don't want a nice girl like that getting mixed up with guys like us."

"We're not bad."

"We're not good either, are we? Do you really want to bring her into our bullshit?"

Patrick wasn't thinking clearly. Sure, we weren't in England anymore but, the past has a way of catching up to you. That was another thing I had learned from my father. "No matter how hard you try to run from it," he'd say. "The past will always catch up to you."

Patrick flops onto the chair next to me. "Well, I'm not gonna tell her, are you?"

"Patrick, she doesn't deserve this."

"But I deserve her." His voice rises in frustration, and I place a hand to his shoulder.

"It's for the best."

Holding the beer between his hands, he leans forward and doesn't say another word.

For the next several days, Patrick dropped the subject of Sara and the Shermans', until one day. Stepping around the front of the Shermans' property, Patrick caught sight of Sara on the porch with a boy. The boy, Jeff, tugged at the pockets of her jeans, forcing her close.

Scoffing at the scene, Patrick returned to his work of snipping shrubs and pulling at dead weeds. When he heard a screech, he looked up and saw the boy with his hand entwined in the girl's hair. Sara squirmed and squealed, fighting against his lips on her face.

Without hesitation, Patrick threw down the shears, then his gloves. When Sara screamed a second time, Patrick broke into a sprint. By the time he arrived on the porch, Jeff had released her and was standing several feet away.

"What the hell are you doing?" Patrick's tone was fierce, and the kid looked scared. "Get the hell outta here." The kid jumped off the porch and into the bush and continued running down the sidewalk.

That was all it took to spark the relationship between Patrick and Sara. Again, I told him to back off.

"This isn't going to work," I said. "She comes from a wealthy family. They have expectations."

Patrick wouldn't listen and four months later he was still trying to convince me to meet her. I refused. It won't last. How could Patrick think otherwise? Did he forget where he came from or the things we've done? It was an impossible relationship, and it was destined to fail.

"Chum." Patrick rushes into the apartment that

afternoon with a big smile on his face. "I just got you the job of a lifetime."

Lying over the sofa, I swivel my glass of brandy in my hand and ask him what the hell he's talking about.

"You'll want to lie down for this."

"I am lying down."

"Sit up, then." He shoves my legs off the couch and sits next to me. "You know that investment firm that the Shermans' own?"

"Yeah."

"Well, they're expanding, and Mr. Sherman is looking to bring in a couple of recruits."

I lean against the couch saying, "Not interested."

"It would be perfect for you."

"No, it wouldn't."

"I told Tom you'd be happy to take the job."

"No, I wouldn't." My gaze is fixed onto his now, but he's still not listening.

"I said you're a great sales guy - incredible with clients."

"What?"

"He wants to meet you." Patrick's eyes and mouth widen simultaneously. "They're expecting you at the house tomorrow evening for dinner."

I sit up straight and look him dead in the eyes. "You did what?"

"Be happy." The grin is still plastered on his face. "This is great for you."

"But I'm not a great salesman. I'm shit. And I hate the damn job."

Patrick waves his hand across the air. "Stuff it, mate.

You're gonna do fine."

The following evening, I find myself seated at the Shermans' dinner table cursing to myself and tugging at the thick material of my new Polo shirt. It's hot in the room, and the piercing glare from the woman seated across the table is making my skin crawl. Not that she's unattractive. With the dark pin-straight hair to her shoulders, the lean face with the high cheekbones, and that perfected figure, the woman is hot. If she wasn't a damn criminal lawyer, I might even be attracted to her.

But Laura, the boss's wife, hadn't stopped eyeballing me since I stepped through the front door. I felt like a prime Grade A bull at the fair with my fresh haircut and shave and the preppy blue shirt. "It's all the rage," the skinny girl at the store had told me. I tug at the shirt again. It's hot as hell is what it is.

Laura buries her laughter into a glass of red wine. I scoff and refill my glass. Maybe I'd made a mistake in coming here. Maybe, I had made a mistake in taking the job altogether.

§

Earlier that evening, after the interview with the boss, I was ushered onto the deck for a cocktail and a cigarette before dinner. There was a chill in the air, but they insisted. While nestled into one of the Shermans' fancy Muskoka chairs on their million-dollar property overlooking their priceless view of the lake, I overheard the evil temptress scolding her husband.

"I don't like him," she shouted from inside the house.

"Laura, please, he can hear you." Tom's tone was quiet, almost muffled, but the woman made no attempt to hide her distaste of me.

"There's something about him," Laura's voice rang out. "I'm telling you, Tom. He reminds me of those clients that strut into the courtroom full of confidence, certain they're going to charm their way to freedom, only to realize that I'm not a cobra."

"Yes, yes, you're the python."

"Don't patronize me, Thomas."

Through the glass doors, I watched as Tom lowered his head and pressed two fingers to the bridge of his nose. "Give him a chance," he said. "He seems like a good guy."

Yes, give me a chance.

"You mean he seems good for business, don't you?" Laura shouted back at her husband.

Thomas Sherman's business partner, Harold Coleman, co-founder of Sherman & Coleman Investments and his wife, Mara, sat out on the deck with me. They were nice people, but they talked my ear off. No doubt, attempting to drown out the sound of the devil-woman's voice – keep the chatter going – bury the background noise. But there was no silencing Laura.

"He's tainted," she ranted on. "Like a wolf in sheep's clothing. How can you not see it?"

She wasn't wrong. I hadn't been honest with anyone since I arrived, not with the landlady, nor the woman at the bank, and certainly not with Tom. But the lies were a means of necessity, and they were better than the alternative because I refused to be hindered by the truth of my past. All I wanted was to be an ordinary guy with an ordinary sort of life. Why couldn't the woman just let me have this?

Then, for the first time, I heard Tom raise his voice. "You don't see the good in him because you don't know him."

"Do you?" Laura huffed back at him. "You know nothing of him besides what little he's told you. What do you really know of this man?"

There was a brief moment of silence. I was certain it was over when I heard her say, "The problem with you, Tom, is that you're always too trusting of everyone. You never see what's right in front of you. And one day, it's going to bite you right in the ass."

There it was. There was the crux. Tom didn't see it because he didn't want to see it, because the prospect of more money was blinding, and why would he want to ruin a good thing?

§

I pull my thoughts back into the room. Laura's gone off somewhere now – thank fuck! I turn my attention to the patio doors, past the deck, the green grass, and the white sands. Then, further still, beyond the fluttering of the tide that washes against the shore. What I wouldn't give to be out there instead of in here. I shut my eyes and take in the cool lake breeze as it fills the room.

"David."

My eyelids swing open. The devil-woman had returned.

"You came over from London with Patrick." It was a statement, not a question. "Did you know that?" She turns to Mara on her left. "Patrick was a boxer over there, and David was his manager."

Jesus, how much did Patrick tell her?

"That sounds exciting," Mara says.

"It wasn't," I grumble.

"And only six months ago," Laura adds. "Isn't that right?"

"Yes," I answer. *What of it?*

Lifting her elbows onto the table, Laura rests her chin onto the palms of her hands. "Fascinating."

"What is?"

"Well, it's just that you don't have much of an accent, is all."

I clench my jaw. I didn't mean to, but it happened, and she saw it. With a steady grin on a stern face, Laura's glare narrows and I swear I can see the devil-horns protruding from her forehead.

"Lydia from the bakery, she's from Sussex, isn't she?" she carries on.

Mara grins politely.

"And that's a heavy accent the woman has. How long has she been here?"

"Twenty years," Mara answers.

I force a grin. It's pre-empted and fake and I don't give a shit. "I guess I've adapted quickly then."

Mara's high-pitched giggle penetrates through the air, but Laura's stiffened expression doesn't falter.

"That's incredible. I mean, really unbelievable. Now, tell me something..." She leans towards me. "How do you suppose that happens?"

Damn patronizing witch. "I'm sure I don't know," I tell her.

"My friend, Keenan, lost his accent after one year," Stephen, the Shermans' youngest, blurts out.

He seems like a good kid, an old soul like his father. I smile across at him, and the kid smiles back.

"That's different, Stephen," Laura tells her son. "Children adapt quicker than adults. And some adults..." Her glare narrows across the table at me. "Some never do."

What the hell was that supposed to mean? I've tried to blend in. I've tried to be like everybody else. What did she know of it? Damn woman, judging my ability to adapt. I'd been adapting my whole damn life!

Sensing my composure slipping away, I rise from my seat, take back the last of my wine, and excuse myself from the table.

Halfway across the room, Tom calls to me. "Hey, David, grab us another bottle of wine from the cooler, will you? Right side..."

Standing at the bathroom mirror, I put a hand to my forehead and wipe off the dampness. What the hell am I doing here? I'm way over my head. And what the hell was Patrick thinking?

With a grunt, I yank the shirt from under my belt. I'm near ready to rip the damn thing clear off. Instead, I reach over to the bathroom window and pull it open.

Looking out to the waves as they ebb and flow, I realize, I could just leave. I could just step out of this bathroom and walk right out the front door. I could just vanish and no one would notice. I've done it before. It would be so easy too, except for that nagging voice at the back of my head telling me to stay. *Do better. Try harder.*

Turning on the tap, I splash cold water on my face and look back in the mirror. All I see is that same hard-ass lying on the cold concrete floor with one foot in the grave. I wasn't going back to that life. There was no way in hell.

Clenching the edge of the sink with my fingers, my body tenses. I need to get a grip.

With a long, slow exhale, I tuck the damn shirt back into my pants and take one last look in the mirror. There's no use in running. I should know better than that.

Defeated, I open the bathroom door and go about my next task.

Stepping into the kitchen, I begin to rummage through the cupboards. I open one door, then another, and then the next. "Where the hell is it?"

"Can I help you?"

The voice startles me and, with alarming speed, I turn around to find her standing in the doorway. She's beautiful, with long waves of dark brown hair, big bright eyes, and that smile...

"Are you lost?" she asks, stepping closer.

"I'm just looking for the wine," I tell her. My throat

feels dry.

Turning towards the cupboard doors, I tell her that Tom asked me to grab a bottle of wine from... I can't remember from where because I'd stopped listening.

She slides an arm past me and opens the cupboard door under the counter to reveal a wine cooler and a collection of bottles.

"Ah." I chuckle to myself, feeling a little foolish. "I was looking up when I should have been looking down."

"It's alright," she says setting a bottle of rosé on the counter. "We all have our weaknesses." She flashes me a smile and I can't help but laugh.

Sara hadn't been at dinner. She was out, her father said. I had felt relieved and yet, somehow, disappointed.

Opening another cupboard door, Sara reaches up into the top shelf and I watch as her summer dress hugs her lean figure.

"You must be David?" she says, her back still to me. When I don't respond, she glances at me just in time to catch my eyes on the back of her dress.

"Yes -" I stumble over my words. "I'm David." *What the hell is wrong with me?*

A soft laugh escapes her and she returns once more to her task. "I'm Sara," she says.

I know that. She's just as Patrick described her, the exact way I had pictured her, the reason I had stayed away.

Setting the glasses on the counter, Sara pops open the bottle of wine as though she's done this a hundred times before. Then, pouring the wine, she hands me one of the glasses.

"What's this for?" I ask.

"You look like you need rescuing."

"Is it that obvious?"

With the sweet smile on her face, she touches her glass to mine. "Cheers."

I return the sentiment and take a drink of my wine, my eyes never leaving hers.

"Issy, you need to stop running away like this."

Seated on an iron bench overlooking the lake, Adrian tells me that what I'm doing, running from my problems, it's a band-aid solution and nothing more. Except that it sure as hell feels right. Why should I sit there listening to my brother's crap about getting my life together? After everything I went through for him, and all those nights spent by his side. Where was he when I needed him.

"Sooner or later, you're going to have to face him, you know?" Adrian now tells me.

"Who are we talking about now?"

"Mike. Eric..." He leans into me. "Your father."

"Ah, all my problems."

Adrian wraps an arm around my shoulders. "Doom and gloom, Issy."

I turn my gaze towards the lake where Sam is standing by the water's edge. I never imagined that, at twenty-one years of age, my life would look like this.

Adrian gives my shoulder a squeeze. "He loves you."

"I know."

"And you love him."

I don't respond.

"Think about it. One day, you could be Mrs. Brick Wall."

I snicker. "Stop."

"Imagine it..." He sweeps a palm across the air. "The white picket fence, the children in the yard, the two-point-five cars. Spectacular."

I nudge him playfully and remind him how much Mike has changed. He wasn't always so controlling. In fact, Mike used to be an easy-going, goofy kind of guy. It was after the incident with Eric in the field that things took a turn. Come to think of it, I didn't use to be this way either.

Adrian shrugs. "Everybody changes."

"He tried to fight you."

"He tried, but he failed."

§

Two weeks after the break-up, Mike called my cellphone. I didn't answer his call, and I refused to respond to his texts. So, one day, he went by the house.

My mother entered my bedroom with a weary look on her face. "Issy, he really wants to talk to you." Apparently, it wasn't Mike's first visit that week.

Lying on my bed, I told her that I didn't want to talk to him. "Just tell him I'm not here."

"I already told him that you are."

"So, lie."

My mother pressed her lips together and glared at me from the doorway.

"Then tell him I just don't want to."

"Issy…"

"Mom."

I don't know what she told him, but Mike went away. Then, two days later, he walked into Rosa's Café with a long-legged woman in a tight dress and tanned skin. I was sitting at a corner table with Adrian and Sam.

Adrian noticed them first. "Wow, he works fast."

I turned to see the woman ogling Mike as they sat together at the other end of the room. He seemed incredibly pleased with himself.

"Asshole."

Adrian said it with vigour, and the woman must have heard him because she whispered something to Mike that made him look our way. It was at that point that I felt Adrian's arm slide across my shoulders. I looked up at him and caught the taunting grimace on his face.

It was all the fuel Mike needed. He shot out of the booth like his ass was on fire. "You have a problem?"

Adrian didn't hold back. "What? It's okay for you but not for her?"

Charged up, Mike reached one powerful arm past my head and took hold of Adrian. Sandwiched between them, I held Mike back. Not that Adrian was trying to avoid him. He was up on his feet with his hands at Mike's collar. All the while, Sam wailed from his seat, begging them to stop.

The incident ended just as quickly as it had begun with Mike hauled out of the shop by a couple of workers. As the door shut behind them, I fell back onto my seat and sighed because, as tough as Adrian is, fighting Mike would have felt a lot like ramming your head into that brick wall.

§

"I don't regret it one bit," Adrian says. "And I'll do it again if I have to."

"That's very sweet of you but -"

"Aw…" Sam, returning to us with his sandals in his hands, wraps his arms around Adrian. "You're such a softy," he says.

I watch them, feeling a little jealous. I want what they have, something sweet and joyful laced with a hint of lust and plenty of love. Mike and I had that before things went wrong.

My cellphone rings, distracting me from my thoughts. Looking down at the screen, I answer with a huff. "What do you want, Eric?"

"Where are you?" he asks.

"At the park with Adrian and Sam."

"Why?"

"Why not?"

"Come to Haddy's," he says. "I have a surprise for you."

I roll my eyes to the sky. We both know how much I love surprises.

"Don't roll your eyes," he says.

I smirk – twin telepathy.

Entering Haddy's pub, I see Eric and Victoria seated at a booth. Across from them are two familiar faces. Smiling, I hurry towards Matt and throw my arms around him - the greatest human ever.

"Hey, kiddo."

"I can't believe you're here." My smile is so big that it hurts.

"It's been a long time," he says.

"Too long." Six months to be exact.

"Hey." The husky voice calls out from behind me and, before I have the chance to turn around, I feel Ben's arms wrap around me and lift me off my feet. "It's my favourite twin."

I laugh.

These are my brother's heroes, the men who saved him and brought him back to me.

Noticing the small protruding belly from underneath Matt's t-shirt, I poke his gut and ask, "What's going on here?"

He chuckles and rubs the bump like he's growing something in there. "I know. I blame Belinda."

"Who's Belinda?"

"My girlfriend," he announces with a bright smile

under dark creamy cheeks. "She's a pastry chef. Gets me to sample all her new creations."

"I'm so happy for you."

"Ah, she's amazing." Ben smacks his hard abs with a solid thud.

"I thought you'd be glad to hear it." Matt smirk and my cheeks flush. The last time I saw Matt, I said some things that weren't very nice. In my defence, I was drunk when I advised him to tell his ex-fiancé to go to hell. The woman accused him of being married to his job. The statement was completely unwarranted; the man saves lives, for goodness sake.

Matt refused to cut back on his hours. Cutting hours meant cutting back on the veterans that required his help, and Matt understood their hardships firsthand. He had watched his father struggle to return to civilian life. For Henry Hamilton, there was little to no assistance for soldiers returning from the Vietnam war.

My brother once said, "The military is great at building soldiers but, damn, do they suck at getting your head back into the civilian body."

Matt's fiancé called him a martyr, took their dog, and left.

As we slide into the booth, we're joined by another couple that I haven't met before. They're part of that clan from the Hamilton-West Centre, Matt tells me.

Ben orders two pitchers of beer along with a round of mugs for everyone, including Eric. My brother isn't supposed to drink. It's a stipulation in his recovery. Today, however, I watch in awe as he fills his glass, takes a gulp, and carries on chatting as though it's all very natural.

Matt leans into me and whispers in my ear. "It's okay. It's under control."

But I continue to stare across the table at my brother, in awe.

"Issy." Matt nudges me with his shoulder. "It's fine. Just leave it alone."

Except that it's not fine. This is so far from fine. Watching Eric with that beer in his hand brings back every single gut-wrenching emotion that I've tried so desperately to eradicate from my mind. How does no one see how wrong this is?

"I kid you not," Ben belts out from the other end of the booth. He's become enthralled in a conversation with the new people. "We were out on Clay Hill that day, out on well-duty, and just as we're approaching, we hear that distinct whistle of a bazooka."

My eyes drift back to Eric as he raises the mug to his lips and I have a sudden urge to lunge across the table and tear the beer from his hand.

"The Humvee takes lift," Ben continues, his voice rising with each word. "It should have blown us all to hell."

My brother nods in agreement.

"The only reason we're still here is because the building we were driving past took on the brunt of the impact." He moves his arms back and forth wildly as he describes the swarm of people fleeing the building. "We rush over to help but realize quickly that the foundation's been compromised. The building's crumbling, but this guy -" Ben motions to Eric. "He goes running in full-tilt and starts pullin' people out."

I've never heard this version of the story before. I knew that there was an explosion. It landed Eric in the hospital for months.

Eric meets my bewildered gaze and quickly looks away again.

"We're telling him to get the hell out of there, but he just keeps running back in. Me and the other guys, we're laying them on the ground. And then, a fire breaks out." Ben lifts his palms and shrugs his shoulders with exaggeration. "Most people would be like, I'm out of here, right? Not this guy. He keeps running in and haulin' em out."

Everyone's laughing, including Eric.

"Until I notice the back of his uniform's on fire. So now, I'm yelling, dude -" Ben cups his hands around his mouth and shouts, "You're on fire. But he won't listen to me. So, I go chasing after him. And do you know what this little shit does? He starts fightin' me."

Eric shakes his head. "Stupid."

"You're not kidding," Ben scoffs. "The only reason that he stopped was 'cause he was nearly unconscious with smoke inhalation. Lucky me, right?" Looking across at Eric, Ben leans back and stretches his arms along the cushions of the seat. "But there he is with one last guy in his arms. He refused to let him go."

"That's incredible," one of the new friends' remarks.

Eric rises with an empty pitcher. "It really isn't."

"Shut up." Ben raises a glass to him. "This right here, folks, this is what heroes are made of."

Eric's grimace fades. "I'm no hero."

"Come on, man. 'Course you are. You don't pull shit like that and then pretend like you didn't do something incredible. You saved a whole ton of people that day. That's hero-worthy shit right there."

An exasperated sigh escapes my brother's throat. "I nearly got you killed."

"Christ. Stop with that shit already."

"I didn't follow protocol. I disobeyed orders." Eric's voice rises. "I was told to stand down, and I refused." His eyes deepen with a look that takes me back to those first days after he returned home. "How heroic is that?" Without another word, Eric turns towards the bar.

"That's bullshit," Ben shouts after him.

"Take it easy on him," Matt remarks. "Don't go undoing everything."

"Please," Victoria utters, her hands clasped together and her eyes glistening.

Ben takes another gulp of beer and slams his mug on the table. As heroic as the story is, its ending remains filled with bitter memories. What followed the rescue on Clay Hill was an onslaught of gunfire from enemy forces that left three soldiers dead along with countless civilians.

Eric sustained burns to his shoulders and upper back. Ben suffered a gunshot wound to the spine that nearly cost him his life. After months of extensive therapy, rehabilitation, and an incredible medical team, Ben walked away with a subtle limp and a lifetime of memories. For both men, the physical damage they sustained healed with time, but their minds continued to betray them.

Ben suffered violent outbursts. It cost him his job and his girlfriend who, he admitted, became terrified to be in the same room with him. Again, it was Matt who came to Ben's rescue. Matt helped to rebuild the broken pieces of Ben's mind, just as he would later do for Eric.

It was also on account of Matt that Ben and Eric were reunited when Matt assigned Ben to be my brother's peer-vet. As a peer-vet, Ben is responsible for Eric. He's supposed to ensure that my brother doesn't fall down any rabbit holes, as Matt put it. Instead, it seemed to me that Ben was pushing my brother in headfirst.

"How can you let him drink?" I hiss at them both. "I thought you were supposed to be looking out for him."

Ben snickers. "Here comes the drama."

"How can you joke about this?"

"Because you're confusing addiction with a need to cope."

I gasp at the absurdity. "Isn't it the same thing?"

"No," he shouts over the music. "It's not."

"Ben," Matt intervenes with the tone of a distraught parent. "You're not helping."

"What?" he motions towards me. "I'm just trying to set things straight because, clearly, she doesn't get it."

I leap off the seat, hitting the top of the table with the palm of my hand. "I'm the one who watched over him when he came back. And I'm the one who was out in that field with him. So, don't you dare tell me that I don't get it. You weren't there. You didn't see what I saw."

I turn and storm across the bar as Ben shouts after me, "I was there – we were all there."

Standing outside the apartment, the cigarette between my lips, I reach through the car's open window and lay on the horn. "Come on, you Irish bastard."

It was nearing seven o'clock in the evening, and I was starting to feel as though my stomach was eating its way through to my spine.

Patrick soon appears on the four-story balcony. His hair is wet with gel and mousse and whatever other concoction Sara has him using this week. She told him that it makes him look like James Dean.

I'd rolled my eyes at him when he said it. "Your girlfriend wants a badass, and you're not it."

Patrick responded with a middle finger in the air.

Now, looking up at him, I shout out, "Stop playing with your damn hair and get down here."

Again, Patrick flips me the middle finger.

"Come on, mate. I'm starving."

"Good," he barks. "Serves you right for being so bloody late."

As he heads back inside, I lean against my new Cutlass sedan, bought off a man who was now too old to drive it. It had been a messy start at Sherman & Coleman Investments. That day, we'd met with an important investor. Tom was over my shoulder throughout the proceedings. In the end, we closed the deal, but the meeting had run an hour and a half longer than expected.

Ten minutes later, pissed off and ready to eat whatever I can find at the corner store, I enter our apartment building and stomp up the stairs.

"What in the hell is keeping him?" I'm cursing to myself again.

Why can't this guy ever be ready on time? Patrick had a problem, I'd decided, the kind that may require therapy. I'd tell him that too. As soon as I got up there, I'd tell him to get some goddamn therapy for his goddamn chronic problem.

Reaching the final flight of stairs, I halt. Our apartment door has been broken into. The wooden frame is cracked and hanging off the hinges. Heart pounding, I race up the stairs, two steps at a time. Inside, I find Patrick lying on the floor with his hands to his abdomen; blood pools between his fingers.

"Damn it." I rush into the kitchen. "Don't move." Grabbing the telephone and a kitchen towel, I hurry to Patrick's side. I press the towel to the wound while I dial 911. Patrick groans.

"What is your emergency?" The woman on the other end of the phone sounds disinterested until I tell her that my friend has been stabbed. "He's bleeding badly. I need an ambulance."

I give her the address, the source of the wound, and describe the intensity of the bleeding. All the while, Patrick's struggling to speak.

"Stop talking," I tell him.

He grabs my wrist and I pull away and concentrate on the wound and the telephone call.

"David…"

The dispatcher tells me the paramedics are on the way.

"David -"

"Stop talking," I hiss.

"It's Devons."

The name sends a chill up my spine. "What did you say?"

"It's him," he gasps, his hand grasping at my shirt. "He's here."

I pull the phone away from my ear. "It's not possible." The man was shot through the head. I saw it with my own eyes. "It can't be him."

Patrick's bloodied hand buckles into a fist. "You need to go to Sara. Go make sure she's okay."

I shake my head at him. I saw the man lying on the floor. He was dead. There was blood everywhere.

His grip tightens. "You and Sara are in danger. You have to go."

Just then, I hear the wail of the sirens. Finally. Damn this city.

"Go." Patrick carries on, his breaths becoming increasingly shallow. "Do you hear me?"

Pressing both hands over the blood-soaked cloth, I listen to the heavy stomps of the paramedic's boots on the stairs. As they enter the apartment, I'm hauled aside, but Patrick's gaze remains locked onto mine. It's that fearful look in his eyes that makes me cave.

Stepping into Rachel's Interior Boutique, I calm the tremble within me just long enough to ask for Sara. The spunky woman behind the counter with the colourful dress smiles with an air of familiarity.

I had been here once or twice before, dropping Patrick off to see Sara. This was before he bought that old pickup truck of his. Patrick said that the truck was an investment because, one day, he'd go into the landscaping business for himself. He just needed some cash for the equipment and a few clients to start with. I told him I'd help with the start-up costs, but he refused handouts.

"It's not a handout, mate," I'd told him. "It's just one brother helping another."

We'd gone back and forth about it. Patrick eventually agreed to some help, saying he'd pay me back every penny. But the way I saw it, I owed him.

"You must be David." Rachel steps around the counter with a peculiar grin. "I've heard a lot about you.

Although…" She places her hands to her curvy hips. "I'd begun to think that you might be an illusion that Patrick and Sara conjured up."

I don't have time for this. "I need to talk to Sara. Is she here?"

"Yes, she's here." She steps closer to me. "Is everything alright?"

I swallow the ache in my throat before explaining that something's happened to Patrick.

"What?" A small whimper pulls my attention to the back of the shop where Sara now stands. "What happened to Patrick?"

I don't know what to say without devastating her. So, I tell her a story that's palatable, about some punk kid who was probably strung out on something.

Sara raises her hands to her mouth and I watch the tears that fill her eyes and spill down her cheeks. I hate this. Why did he make me come here?

"Is he going to be okay?" Rachel asks.

"I don't know. He's been taken to the hospital. I'm on my way there now."

Sara turns to her aunt. Rachel embraces her and tells her to hurry along.

Patrick had been rushed into surgery. He was lucky, we'd been told. The knife had missed his vital organs. Patrick would recover.

After surgery, we're ushered into a room where Patrick lies with his eyes half-open. Sara rushes to his side. Holding his face in her hands, she kisses him.

"Are you alright?" she asks. "Do you feel any pain?"

His voice is quiet and sluggish. "I'm alright." He takes her hands into his and his eyes drift towards mine. "Thank you," he says.

I nod.

Seated at his side, Sara asks about the attack. She wants to know everything: the man's face, the words exchanged. I answer her questions on Patrick's behalf, continuing with the lie I'd started earlier. Patrick nods in agreement and says little.

Then, as Sara leaves to use the washroom, Patrick waves me over. "Did you find anything?" he asks.

"Patrick..."

"Keep looking," he says. "He's bound to turn up."

I take a deep breath. "This is absurd."

"Look," he huffs at me. "You don't have to believe me. If I'm wrong, then all the better. But if I'm right, then you're gonna thank me, aren't you?"

I left the hospital feeling agitated and thinking that Patrick was losing his mind.

Three days later, I arrive home from work, change out of my work clothes, and prepare to head over to the hospital when I hear a loud knock at the newly patched-up apartment door. Looking through the peephole, I find Sara standing there, red-faced and glossy-eyed.

I open the door.

"He's gone," she cries.

"Gone? What do you mean gone?"

Sara steps inside and grabs onto me. "I went to the hospital. Patrick isn't there." She exhales into a sob. "No one knows where he is."

I rush towards Patrick's bedroom and throw the door open. The drawers from his dresser are pulled open and his clothes are scattered over the bed and floor. Inside the single drawer of his nightstand, I find Patrick's wallet is gone, along with a switchblade that he never uses, and his passport.

Then, turning towards the closet, I notice that the duffle bag he'd brought over from England is also missing. What the hell is he doing?

The Keeper of Things

Part II

Chapter 9   August 2016

One year ago, I came to learn that Eric was diagnosed with severe depression and PTSD. By April of 2015, my brother had been in therapy for more than a year. It wasn't working.

That same month, winter's end dumped an additional three feet of snow on the ground. Arriving home from University, I noticed that my brother's pickup truck was gone and, as I entered the front door of our home, I was instantly hit with the pungent odour of liquor. I followed the stench through the living room and into my father's office. There, I saw the broken lock of the liquor cabinet and the shattered bottle of whiskey on the floor. Above the cabinet, the remnants of alcohol stained the wall.

I called Mike and we raced out to the field. At this point, our relationship was already suffering. Between the sleepless nights spent worrying about my brother and the reality that we might very well lose him, Mike and I spent little time together. When we were together, it was mostly on Eric-related errands.

Arriving at the barn, its wooden siding discoloured in a hue of rusted brown, we found Eric's pickup parked on the gravel driveway with the passenger door wide open. Ahead, the snow-covered field glistened under the sunlight.

Mike stepped forward and, shielding his eyes from the sun, he scoured the area. I stood next to him, mimicking his pose. That's when I caught sight of the still figure hunched in the distance. I remember the cold chill that washed over me, the feeling that we were already too late.

Suddenly, Eric lifted his arm and the dark object in his hand moved towards his head. The shrilling sound that erupted from me sent Mike racing into the field. I set off after him, crying out to Eric and pleading with God to make him stop.

Mike reached him first and, from several feet away, I watched as Mike tumbled into Eric. Pinning my brother to the ground, Mike fought to pry the gun from Eric's hand. The weapon wavered back and forth. I held my breath. At last, the gun was tossed into the snow, but Eric refused to give in.

With furious determination, my brother clawed his

way towards the weapon. I moved forward, panic rising, just as Mike caught Eric by the legs and hauled him back. In a final moment of desperation, Eric turned onto his back. With rage on his face and tears in his eyes, he lunged forward and struck Mike across the face.

"What the hell is the matter with you?" Mike shouted as he shook him. "What are you thinking?"

I stood over them, begging them to stop but Eric continued to fight. It was then that Mike clenched his fist tight and struck Eric. The fight was over.

We sat by my brother's side for some time afterwards, while Eric lay over the snow with his forearm over his eyes and tears running down the sides of his face.

I can still recall the agony in my brother's voice that day as he begged us to just let him die. It tore me apart.

After the incident, we drove to my uncle's house. Eric begged us not to take him home. He couldn't face my parents.

Stephen was waiting on his driveway when we arrived at the house. He wrapped his arms around my twin and told him, "You're going to be right again."

Eric lowered his head. I presumed then that it was out of regret or shame. I would come to understand that what Eric felt at that moment had nothing to do with either.

Matt arrived at the house before nightfall. He spent hours talking to Eric while the rest of us sat in the kitchen, impatiently waiting. The hope that day was that Eric would agree to go with Matt to the Centre. There, my brother would receive the care he needed, surrounded by people who knew what he was going through. Eric listened, and then he slept.

When we received the news that he had agreed to go to Ottawa, we were, of course, grateful and relieved. Until we heard the front door slam shut. Stephen ran out first, followed by Mike and Matt.

By the time I arrived on the front porch, Eric was lying face down on the driveway.

"Look, man," Matt shouted. "I've seen plenty of guys go down this path, and it doesn't usually end well."

"I don't give a shit," Eric fought to free himself and Mike tightened his grip around him.

"You can't do this alone," Matt told him.

"I didn't ask for your help."

"Well, you're getting it anyway."

"Go to hell." Eric snarled. "You think you're helping me? You think you're gonna make me better? Fix me? You can't help me. Assholes."

I looked on with tears in my eyes as my brother continued to struggle, his face pressed to the ground.

"This is bullshit," he shouted.

Stephen wrapped his arm around me. "Don't worry," he said. "He'll tire out soon enough."

"Look." Matt crouched onto one knee. "I know you feel like you're so far down that rabbit hole that you'll never climb back out, but I'm telling you that you're wrong. Let me prove it to you."

Eric refused.

It was then that Matt glanced over at me, then to my uncle. With a single nod from Stephen, Matt rose saying, "Alright, here's the alternative. If you refuse to go to the Centre, your next trip is straight to the psych ward at the nearest hospital. And when they discover that you're a risk to yourself, you'll be sent to a facility where you'll spend many, many months convincing a whole bunch of people that you're not suicidal, that you value your life. But I can almost guarantee you that they won't believe you because I sure as hell don't. So, what do you say? Will you let me help you?"

Several minutes passed in silence. It felt like an eternity but, just as Stephen predicted, Eric stopped struggling, and Mike eased his grip.

Two days later, Eric arrived at the Hamilton-West Centre in Ottawa. I was there with him in those first days. I tried to explain that my brother wouldn't want me there but, Matt assured me that I was mistaken.

"He'll need you there for support," he said.

The Centre, a long, single-story building, was situated at the end of a quiet suburb. Inside, Matt led us down a sterile-looking corridor.

The sign on the door read 'Room B.' When Eric entered, the colour flushed from his face. In the centre of the room, where twelve folding chairs were positioned in a circle, sat Ben Peterson.

Seeing his friend there, healthy and able, it changed everything.

The conversation that afternoon began with mild chatter. Ben cracked a few jokes and Eric even laughed a little. But I could see the discomfort on my brother's face. He didn't want to be in that room any more than I did. Instead, Eric's focus continuously reverted towards the large square window at the end of the room as though looking for an escape.

When Matt finally asked my brother to begin, Eric asked, "What do you want to know?"

"Tell me what keeps you up at night?"

Eric's jaw tightened. "That's a loaded question, don't you think?"

"That's why we're here."

"How about we start instead with all the reasons why I don't want to be here?"

Ben chuckled, and Matt said, "That would be counter-productive, don't you think?"

Eric didn't respond.

"Alright." Matt leaned forward and, resting his elbows on his knees, he said, "Why don't you tell me what happened on Clay Hill?"

"Man..." My brother's gaze lowered to his lap. "You want me to get into this now?"

"Yes, sir," Matt answered. "That's why we're here."

Ben nudged my brother with an elbow saying, "That's how we do it here. You talk, we listen."

"I don't want to talk about this shit."

"You're doing yourself a great disservice then," Matt urged.

"I agree," Ben said. "You should talk about it. Tell people what happened to you – what happened to us."

"People should know," Matt added. "Your family should know." He looked across at me in that sympathetic way of his.

A long moment of silence followed. Then, with a slow, sluggish shrug, Eric began. He said, "People keep telling me that what I did, going out there, risking my life, that it makes me heroic. It's all bullshit." He turned to Ben. "What we did out there, it doesn't make us heroes."

"We did what we had to do," Ben stated.

"Did we?" There was a scowl on my brother's face. "How many people died because of what we did? Or what we didn't do?" He then turned his attention to Matt. "You want to know why I went out to that field?"

I stared across at him, my heart racing.

"I wanted to make it all go away. No more thoughts. No more memories. That's why I went out there."

The room fell silent, and I couldn't help the tears that filled my eyes.

Matt leaned back into the chair and I focused on his grey suede sneakers. "Tell me what made you go out to the field," he said, quieter than before.

Once again, my brother turned his gaze towards the window. Then, Eric told us his story.

Chapter 10   April 1991

Pulling up to the lake, I turn off the ignition to the old sedan and roll down the windows. Leaning into the seat, I take in the cool breeze. Sara's sobs have subsided. She had been reading Patrick's letter and now, she was silent.

'I screwed up badly,' Patrick wrote. 'There's no turning back from this. I wish I could have seen you one last time, to hold you, and tell you how much you mean to me. Maybe one day, we'll see each other again. For now, you'll have to get on without me.

Tell your family that I've found a great job out west, that it's much too good to pass up. They'll like that, and I'd hate *for them to think that I've left without a word.*

And Sara, please don't hate me for this. I can't tell you why I have to go. Just know that I'm doing this for you. I'm sorry.

Patrick'

The crumbling of paper pulls my attention back into the car and I turn to find the letter rolled up into Sara's fists. She tosses the letter and picks up the envelope.

I retrieve the wrinkled letter down by her feet and smooth it out with the palms of my hands while Sara examines the yellow-stained envelope.

"When did you get this?" she asks, holding the envelope in the air.

"I found it in the mailbox this morning," I tell her.

"There's no return address. Or a stamp." She shakes the envelope at me. "He delivered it himself?"

"I don't know."

"Well, how else could it have been delivered?"

Once again, I tell her that I don't know.

She slaps the envelope onto my lap. "I'm so tired of this bullshit."

I had never heard her swear before and it sounds strange coming from her gentle lips.

"And I'm so tired of both of you and your damn secrets." Her voice wavers and, without warning, Sara breaks down. With her hands to her face, her shoulders shaking, she leans over her lap and sobs.

"Hey..." I reach out to her and place a gentle hand to her back, but I have no words to console her. What am I supposed to say to her, that everything is going to be okay, that Patrick will come back? It isn't true and I don't believe it. The truth is that Patrick called two days ago saying he was heading across the country towards the Atlantic coast.

§

"Are you out of your fucking mind? Get back here before you do something stupid."

Patrick had called me from a phone booth close to the border of Quebec. He was out of his mind.

"It's alright," he said. "The plan's working."

"Plan? What plan?" I picked up the phone and began pacing from the kitchen to the living room, as far as the cord would go.

"David. Listen." He was almost inaudible at times, whispering through short pauses. "I made sure he followed me out of the city."

"Patrick." I was losing my mind. "What the hell are you talking about?"

"Devons - he was at the hospital."

That name, it continued to send a chill through me.

"He walked right past my room. He was looking for me. So, as long as he's following me, you and Sara are safe."

"The man is dead, Patrick. He's dead. You shot him. Do you remember that?" I shouted through the phone. It was all I could do to avoid punching another hole in the wall.

"No, damn it. He's alive." The sudden outburst was

instantly followed by a moment of deafening silence.

Patrick's sighting of Devons was unfathomable. We were both there in Barton's estate that day. The man couldn't have survived the head wound, and I'd become skeptical of Patrick's insistence that it was the same man who attacked him at the apartment. It just isn't possible.

"Look," Patrick's voice became quiet and calm once again. "I know you don't believe me, and I know you think I'm losing my mind. But I know what I saw, David. It's him. Just tell Sara that I'm sorry about all of this."

"She knows you're sorry."

"Tell her again. Please."

The phone went dead, and I was left standing there listening to the dial tone and feeling completely helpless. But I promised myself that I would tell her, even though I was certain that Patrick was delusional. Perhaps suffering from some sort of psychotic episode, like soldiers in times of war who suffered terribly from traumatic experiences during battle as they watched friends and brother's parish right before their eyes. Shell shock is what they called it, post-war neurosis brought on by hysteria, concussions, and trauma.

§

I turn to Sara and, with my hand still pressed to her back, I tell her, "I'm sorry."

Sara leans her head against my shoulder. I can feel the dampness from her tears, and it makes my heart ache.

I touch my lips to the top of her head but, just as suddenly, I pull away. "I should take you back," I tell her.

Sara doesn't say a word. She eases herself against the seat, turns her face towards the passenger window, and remains that way until we arrive at the boutique.

As I pull up to the curb, Sara opens the car door and hurries into her aunt's shop. With a long sigh, I move around the vehicle and close the passenger door that's been left wide open.

"David."

The sharp voice startles me and I turn around to find Rachel standing behind me with a fierce glare on her face.

"What on earth did you do to her?"

"It's not what you think." Reaching into my jacket pocket, I pull out the wrinkled paper and hand it to her. "Here."

"What's this?"

"A letter from Patrick."

While Rachel reads through the letter, I pull out my cigarette pack and light one up.

"Thanks." Rachel yanks the cigarette from my lips and takes a long puff.

I grimace and light another one.

"Hm," she murmurs through pressed lips.

"What is it?"

With one eye partially closed from the cigarette smoke, she says, "Sara told me that Patrick didn't like to talk about his past." She returns the letter to me and her eyes fix onto mine. "And, anytime he did, there were all sorts of holes in his stories. She said he was hiding something. Something big."

Sensing the accusation, I drop my gaze from hers.

"David, what's going on?"

"Like I told Sara, he did something that he shouldn't have done, and now he's paying for it."

"Look." Rachel's tone becomes stern. "I like you, David, despite Laura's warnings and all your loose ends. But this -" she points her cigarette towards the shop's window. "This is not okay." Then, turning the lit cigarette on me, she says, "You're going to tell me what's going on, or else, whatever this is between you and Sara, it's going to end."

Staring down at the searing end of the cigarette, I lean against my car. As much as I don't want to bring up the past, I get the feeling that I'm not going to get out of this one, not with Rachel.

I take a deep breath and then, I tell her as much as is necessary. I tell her about Barton, the fights, the concussions, and the need to pull Patrick away from it all.

Then, I tell her of the days spent in the basement of Barton's estate. I'd never told anyone about that. Finally, I tell her about Devons and how, on that final day, Patrick came into the house with a couple of guys.

"He shot Devons to protect me." I look down at the ground, the memory still fresh in my mind. Patrick had never shot anyone before. "Now, he thinks Devons is after him."

"And you don't?"

"No, it's absurd. The man's dead."

"What if you're wrong?"

I grumble at the thought. If Devons is indeed alive, then Patrick has no hope on earth or in hell of escaping the man.

Blowing a steady stream of smoke between puckered lips, Rachel asks, "And where is Patrick now?"

"I don't know. But Patrick needs to get his ass back here before he gets himself hurt."

"Well, it this Devons person is indeed alive, and Patrick is trying to avert this man's attention away from you and Sara, then, it seems to me that he's just trying to be a friend. A damn good one."

"He's being stupid." I turn my face away. "I should have never got him mixed up in this." It's my biggest regret.

With a grin, Rachel throws her cigarette onto the ground and butts it out with the tip of her shoe. "You know, this is what I like about you," she says. "Underneath all that muscle and the foreboding glare, you have a heart."

I take a final puff of my cigarette and toss it.

"And you know what else?"

"What?"

"You remind me a lot of myself when I was your age."

"How's that?"

"This no bullshit attitude of yours. I was like that once." She shrugs. "I've softened over the years."

She still didn't give a crap what people thought of her, that much was clear. I admired her for that.

"And just for the record..." Rachel leans in close. "Laura didn't like me very much at the beginning either. She warmed up to me, eventually. Truth be told, she doesn't like anybody at first glance." She chuckles. "It's the job, I think. Anyhow, I wouldn't worry too much about Patrick. If he's been on his own as long as you say, then he'll be fine."

If only Patrick knew what the hell he was doing.

Then, unexpectedly, Rachel reaches out and pats me on the shoulder. "And don't worry, English," she says with a smile. "Your secrets are safe with me."

I smile back at her, thankful for her friendship. Through the shop's window, I see Sara moving about the shop. "Maybe I should go in and talk to her."

"Give her time," Rachel tells me.

I take a deep breath, but I do as she requests. I give Sara the time she needs to come to terms with her new reality.

The following day, instead of going by the shop, I call.

"She didn't come in today," Rachel tells me.

I sigh and, as though reading my mind, she says, "Don't worry. She'll come around."

"Tom asked about Patrick," I tell her.

"What did you say?"

"I told him exactly what was on the letter. I said that he'd come by a job offer that he couldn't refuse and that it could potentially become permanent."

"That's a good story. Covers all the bases."

"I suppose. But I'm tired of all the lying."

"Well, you could tell him the truth. Although, like

you said, considering the alternative, I think you're making the right choice."

She's right. Of course, she's right. How can I possibly tell them the truth? I was being irrational. I wasn't thinking straight. It isn't like me.

But I guess that's why we get along so well, because she's capable of being rational, and she doesn't seem to allow emotions to overcloud judgement. Mostly, Rachel's genuine, and that's a rare quality. Most people only present the version of themselves that they want others to see, myself included. With my high-end suits and the well-paying job, I appear to be the guy who has it all figured out. What no one sees are the scars hidden underneath the fancy suits nor the burdens of the past buried in the patched-up holes of my apartment walls.

No one knows about the fighting that still goes on from time to time, somewhere deep in the pits of the city, or in the alleyways of some dive bar. Nor the bruises and cuts that I cover up with yet more lies.

No one sees that. All that people see are the lies. It's for this reason that I admire Rachel. She presents the truth of herself for all to see. She doesn't feel the need to put on a show for others, to hold back when she has something to say, or pretend to be something she's not. It's for these reasons that I accept her threats and her friendship.

"She's here today," Rachel tells me when I call again the next day. Except, this time, it's Rachel who's sighing.

"She came in here with a frown, slammed the front door behind her, and tossed her bag over her workstation. Now, she's throwing things around in the back." Rachel huffs. "I guess that's progress though, right?"

"Progress?"

"You know, the signs of grieving. She's getting it all out." I hear a thud in the background. "Maybe tomorrow will come acceptance, and my shop might be saved." She chuckles a little, but it's lost in another sigh

By the end of the week, Rachel tells me that Sara seems less agitated. "She looks happier," she says.

I'm relieved until Tom tells me that Sara's been spending most of her time in her bedroom.

"She seems down," he says. "She doesn't want to talk to anybody. She just wants to be left alone in her room. And she isn't eating much either..." He shrugs. "I guess it's expected. These things take time."

Concern fills me once again.

"It was warmer than usual that day. It was mid-day, April 2015, and there was three feet of snow on the ground. I sat in my truck for a while with the windows rolled down and a bottle of Jack Daniels in my hand.

That field, that's the place I go to be alone. To think and get drunk without prosecution. No one knows about that place." My brother looked across the room at me. "Except for you and Mike. But you didn't care for it, did you? No one cares about it. No one appreciates it like I do, the solidarity and quietness of the place. Just like no one understands why I'll never be how I used to be - normal.

Isn't that what they say when they talk about me?

How much I've changed, how different I behave and look. How I'm not normal?" Eric scoffed. "They like to use that word a lot, don't they? Back to normal. Back to the way things were before. Everything back to normal. There's something cynical in it, isn't it? As though everyone else is abnormal. Well..." Eric reached into his pocket and pulled out a pack of cigarettes and the shiny metallic Zippo lighter that he carries around.

"You can't smoke in here," Matt told him.

Eric lit up anyway.

Seated next to Matt in the circle in Room B, I watched my brother's hardened glare fix onto Matt's. "I sure as hell don't feel normal." He blows the smoke out through pressed lips. "I don't even recognize myself anymore. What do you suppose that means, doc?"

"I'm not a doctor," Matt told him.

"Then what are you? A head shrink?"

"I'm a therapist. For Veterans, like you."

"Ah." Eric takes another puff. "You're a social worker.

"Yes."

"But you've never been to war, have you?"

Matt shakes his head. "I don't need to have been through a war to know how it affects the mind."

Eric scoffed once again and turned to Ben at his side. "And you're okay with this?"

Ben flashed my brother a half-smile and said, "He's very good at what he does. Believe me, I know."

My brother lowered his head and took another puff of his cigarette.

No, Eric wasn't the same because the person I saw seated in that pale-coloured room was a broken man, a man filled with pain and torment and guilt. The boy that we remembered was gone. He had turned into a man, and that man that the army built into a soldier had been left behind in the mountains of Afghanistan.

"You see," Eric then said. "I never came back. I'm still out there." He pointed towards the large square window, the lit cigarette between his fingers. "That's where the real me is. Buried somewhere out there with all those that died. So, how can I be normal? But war has a way of changing people, doesn't it?"

"Yes, it does," Matt agreed with a gentle smile. "So, tell me what happened next?"

"Well, I took a drink, and then I took another, and then another." My brother grinned. "But there was a purpose to it. I knew that, soon, it would be over. I just needed to numb my mind a little."

"Why did you feel that it needed to be over?"

"See, you don't get it. You say you do, but you don't." Eric's voice rose and fell again. "Stephen got it," he added with a subtle nod. "He took me out to Burlington one day to see the World War Two Memorial. There were hundreds of names engraved into the stone. So much death."

If that IED hadn't taken out Stephen's men and left him with an empty sleeve, would he be normal? I wonder how Stephen and Eric would be if things had gone differently.

My brother was sent home with a list of medications and another list of therapist's names. He cringed with every visit, he told me. "How can they possibly help me if I can't even explain what the hell I'm feeling?" he said.

"Why did you stop going to therapy?" Matt asked.

Looking out the window, Eric said, "In my last session, I asked the therapist, "Why the hell did I get to live? Why didn't I die out there with the rest of them? Why was I allowed to come home?" She told me it was guilt. "Survivor's guilt," is what she called it." He turned his glare back onto Matt's saying, "I didn't need some damn therapist to tell me that. I know what I'm feeling. What I need is to make it stop."

My brother jabbed his index finger to the side of his head and his eyes went dark. "The guilt festers in my brain like a parasite looking for a warm soft spot to lay its eggs and I can't make it stop."

"I can help you," Matt told him.

"Can you?" The taunting smirk returned to my brother's face.

"Yes, I can."

"He helped me," Ben remarked, and Eric tossed the cigarette onto the tiled floor.

"I don't have any right to complain about my life," he said staring down at the cigarette as it began to die out. "Not when there are so many that had theirs taken away." He took a deep breath. "And yet, here I am feeling unworthy of it."

"Is that what you think?" Matt asked. "That you're unworthy of your life?"

Eric fought against shameful tears. "You know, they keep saying that it'll get better, that the dark feelings will pass, but they lie."

Stephen had put it into perspective though. He said, "I'm not going to tell you that everything's going to be okay, or that the bad feelings will go away, or that the nightmares will stop. One day, you'll come to terms with your memories. You'll learn to accept them for what they are. And then you'll begin to heal, and you will learn to live again." But not even Stephen could make the thoughts go away.

"So, I gulped at that whiskey bottle until the mickey was almost empty, until my mind grew numb and my thoughts stopped racing. Then, I reached under my seat and touched the cold metal, but I paused. It was only a moment of hesitation, but it was there."

"What made you pause?"

"I was thinking... but the moment passed."

"Thinking about what?"

Eric hesitated. "About that day, on Clay Hill."

"Tell me about it."

That day, there was a terrible stench in the air, my brother told us. He couldn't make it out. The fire had begun to engulf the building. Eric reached out to take hold of another body, and the skin on his hands felt like it was melting away. The fire was spreading fast.

Burnt flesh. That's what it was. That was the smell. Burnt flesh mixed with the toxic gas from the explosion. The stench of it had become lodged into his brain, just like the guilt.

The helicopters descended upon them in a cloud of dust. They were ordered to take those that could be recovered.

"It was the most dreadful order I'd ever received," he said. One that would torment him his entire life. Men cried out for help, trying desperately to get his attention, pleading for one brief moment of human compassion from anyone willing to stop and pick up their mutilated bodies and carry them out of there. There were women and children too... their bodies lying limp. They couldn't be saved. They would remain there in the dirt and rubble.

"Bauer. Get the hell out of there." The Sergeant was shouting at him. "The structure isn't stable." He heard his commanding officer loud and clear, but he couldn't leave those people to die. They didn't deserve this.

He went in again and again, until Ben was at his back, slapping his uniform. "You're on fire. Get out!" Eric was hurt. His hair, his uniform, his face, all blackened by the smoke. He could feel his lungs giving out. Soon, he was being carried out of the building.

"There are civilians in there," he struggled to speak. But bullets were flying. Ben was hit. His eyes stared out, empty. When Ben's legs gave out, both men dropped to the ground.

Eric saw the small hole in the front of his friend's uniform and the thin trail of bright red blood that trickled from the wound. It tore straight through his body. Eric tried to call out for help, but he could hardly breathe. His lungs were filled with smoke, and he coughed violently as the shells continued to fly past them.

Then, everything went dark.

"I woke up in a military hospital outside of Kabul. I'd been unconscious for days, the doctor said. That's when the memories began to flood in. Memories of the dead, and those left behind. If only I'd had more time." He'd turned his gaze to Ben then and uttered, "I'm sorry. If I'd just listened. If I had just followed orders."

"Stop," Ben tells him.

"No." Tears filled my brother's eyes. "I almost got you killed."

Eric was sent to one hospital and Ben to another. It would be months before he'd hear from his friend again, before he'd learn that Ben was still alive, and in that time the guilt and torment ate away at his mind. The others... they would return in wooden boxes.

Eric closed his eyes and waited for the tremble to subside. He hadn't been prepared for the things he'd witnessed, the destruction, the devastation, the continuous sounds of gunfire and heavy artillery. The sounds still rattled his eardrums and caused him to tremble.

Not anyone, nor any single thing, could save him from what he felt. That's what he'd told us that day. Not the pills, not Stephen. Of course, there was the alcohol but even that only masked the ache. Maybe Victoria could have helped him. She had eased his mind, even if for a while.

"So, I took a final swig of the whiskey and dropped to my knees." He opened his hand wide and stared down at his palm. "I looked at the pistol in my hand, trying to remember when the thought first came to me. It happened one day, somewhere around the time that the shaking began, after that incident." One corner of his mouth rose. "Ironic that that weapon should be my saviour."

"That was how you'd resolved to escape the nightmares?" Matt asked.

"I've been through months and months of head shrinks and pills and endless mention of rest. I've had enough. All I want is for it to end. I need the torment and the damn nightmares to end."

However, the decision wasn't without its regrets, he said. He would never tell his family goodbye, nor explain why he felt the need to end his life. He could only hope that we would come to understand, and to forgive.

My brother had looked at me then as my eyes clouded over with tears. "All I wanted was for you to understand and accept my decision - understand that this isn't a life worth living."

The thought of it still brings tears to my eyes.

§

"Issy..." The door to Haddy's pub opens, and Matt comes to stand in front of me with another one of his sympathetic looks. "I'm so sorry, Issy."

I've been standing here, outside of Haddy's pub with my thoughts stuck on that day in Room B, the horrible day when Eric told us his story. It tore me apart.

With tears in my eyes, I extend my hand towards the pub's doors, asking "How can you allow him to drink again? After everything he's been through."

I'm shouting, and the people passing by on the

other side of the road turn to look at us.

"I know." Matt places a hand on my shoulder, and I shrug him off. "But, Issy, Eric's come such a long way. He's nothing like he was a year ago. Not even six months ago."

"I know that." Does he think that I don't know that? I remember all of it.

When my brother told us of the tragedy that occurred on Clay Hill, I remember the darkness that came into his eyes. That's when I knew that my brother too had become tarnished by the inhumanness of war. It was unforgiving. It did not discriminate. And Eric had not escaped its cruelty.

"To watch helplessly while fellow soldiers and friends and civilians die," he told us, "Those are the tragic events that leave their scars."

Matt would later tell me that my brother doesn't want to die. What Eric wants is peace.

"If someone told him, I can take away the bad thoughts and those haunting memories, do you think he'd still choose death? What Eric wants," Matt said, "Is for all the chaos in his head to stop."

It was all a desperate attempt to erase the past.

Now, as I look at Matt's dark complexion, I can't help but feel a sense of betrayal. "You, of all people, know how much he's struggled. Ben doesn't know the whole story. He wasn't there. You were."

"Issy." His tone is firm but, as always, there is a node of sympathy in his voice. "You've got to trust me on this."

Right. I've heard this all before; the pleas for trust, the promises of assurance.

"Listen," Matt utters, and I bury my hands into my pockets and stare mindlessly down at his grey suede sneakers. "I know you're proud and stubborn like your brother." He grimaces, trying to ease the tension. It's not working. "But I think you should talk to someone."

I flash him a hard look.

"If you're not comfortable talking to anyone else, then talk to me. You know you can trust me. Maybe..." He leans in closer. "You might even write about it someday."

I clasp the house keys tight in my fist until it hurts. There have been so many episodes with Eric, episodes that left him jarred and unable to cope. Matt knew it; Ben knew it too. So, how can they allow my brother to fall down that hole again?

"What do you say?" he asks.

"Just do your part," I snap. "Take care of my brother." Without another word, I turn around and walk away.

Storming through the front door of Rachel's shop, I'm instantly met by the woman's glare.

"David." She steps around the counter. "I told you -"

"I know." I raise my palm to her. "I'm sorry. I can't anymore." I know I shouldn't be here, but I have to see her.

"David." A small voice calls out to me and I turn to find Sara standing at the end of the room. I move towards her and Sara steps into my embrace.

"Do you want to get out of here?" I ask.

She nods, and I turn to Rachel. "We won't be long."

Rachel widens her eyes at me, as though signalling a warning. I know she's concerned, and why wouldn't she be? If things went so wrong with Patrick, how could they possibly be any different with me?

Seated in my car, Sara holds her head low.

"Are you okay?" I ask.

She turns to look at me, her frown intensifying. "No. Where have you been?"

"What do you mean?"

"You just... disappeared. I needed you. You're the only person I can talk to about this, and you just..." She throws her arms up in frustration, "Vanished."

I didn't know what to say. I thought I was doing the right thing in giving her space. Wasn't that what Rachel told me to do? "I thought you needed time, space."

"Whatever." She turns her face away from mine. "Can we just go to your place?"

"Are you sure?"

Staring ahead, she nods.

Stepping onto the balcony of my apartment I hand Sara a cold bottle of beer. "Your aunt's going to kill me for this."

She leans against the railing. "She doesn't need to know."

"She'll smell it on you."

"It doesn't matter." She turns to me then with an unjustified glare. "And aren't you supposed to be at work?"

"I left early."

"Why?"

I had to see you. That day, I told Thomas I had an important appointment but, truthfully, I was going mad. After he told me that Sara wasn't eating, that she was down, that is was normal for young women to feel this way, I knew I had to see her. It isn't normal, and it isn't okay.

"I had to make sure you were alright," I tell her.

Sara rolls her eyes at me and takes a seat on one of the new wooden chairs. "Took you long enough."

I sit next to her and sip at my beer the way that I used to do with Patrick... *I should have gone after him – I should have demanded to know where he was – I should have tried harder.*

I take a deep breath. "You know, I wasn't going to give you that letter."

Sara turns to me with an accusatory frown, and I take another sip of my beer before explaining, "I wanted to wait, see if he'd give me more to go on."

She scoffs at the remark. "Well, I'm glad you did, otherwise, I'd still be here waiting around like an idiot." She leans back, folds her arms tight across her chest, and throws one leg over the other the way her mother does. "This way, I won't waste any time in getting over him." She swallows the bitterness of those words before adding, "Besides, they say knowing is half the battle, right? So, the more I know, the easier it will be for me to move on."

I watch her for a moment, the pink of her cheeks, the pout of her lips, the sadness in her eyes. Then, setting my bottle down, I begin to unfasten the buttons of my dress shirt.

Sara turns to me with a curious raise of her eyebrows. "What are you doing?"

I pull on the collar of the shirt and expose my

wounds.

Sara leans towards me. "What happened?"

At the base of the neck, close to the left shoulder, three distinct markings come together in the shape of a triangle. These are the remnants of the past.

"Burn marks. Cigarettes."

"Does it hurt?"

"No."

Reaching out with the tips of her fingers, she traces the scars. "Who did this to you?"

Taken aback by her touch, I adjust the collar. "The same guy that's after Patrick." I do up the buttons and turn to face her.

Sara's gaze widens. "You're saying the man who did this to you is..." Her voice cracks. "That's why he left?"

It's bad. I know it's bad, but what the hell was I supposed to do? I don't know where the hell Patrick is, or why he's doing this, or where he's headed. I don't even know if Devons is really alive. For the first time since the incident at Barton's estate, I feel completely powerless and there's nothing I can do about it.

"I'm sorry that you're stuck in this mess," I tell her. "He should have never brought you into this."

Unexpectedly, I feel Sara's hand on my shoulder. "You didn't do this to him," she says. "You didn't make him leave."

I clench my jaw. If only that were true. "I wish I could help him." I swallow the ache in my throat. "If I knew where he was..."

Her hand moves further across my neck and comes to rest on the spot where the scars are seared into my skin.

"I'm sorry that you've lost your friend," she tells me. "But this is not your fault."

The words cause an ache in my chest. In my life, it had been rare that anyone should care for me, let alone notice what I'm feeling.

"David." The gentleness in Sara's voice forces me to halt my thoughts. "We'll get through this, together."

Once again, I'm stunned by her. This girl, this woman, she's continuously challenging my patience and my emotions. At one moment, frustrating me beyond belief and, in the same breath, she'll say something so sweet, do something so unexpected that it throws me off. A smile, a subtle touch, the sweetest words, it was all it took to make me stop and think and readjust. I can't understand it. How can this woman hold so much power over me? This was precisely why I had told Patrick to keep her away, because one moment alone with Sara, and I was in love.

High up on the sixth floor of the nineteenth-century building, I look out the window to the ocean ahead. Past the narrow roadway, the train track, and the sandy beach, the ocean waves swell and crash against the stone wall barrier. A sudden gust blows past me, and the storm surge pushes the water inland. Thirty-foot waves rush towards the building. I slam the wooden shutters together and recoil into the safety of the apartment.

Moments later, I return to the window. The water has receded and now, snow fills the streets. Below, a man lies face down. He has waves of light brown hair and wears a dark jacket and blue jeans. Red markings speckle the soft tuft of freshly fallen snow around him.

I wake up in a cold sweat. This dream has plagued me for years. After the incident with Eric in the field, I'd come to think of the dream as an omen of what was to come. When I had mentioned it to Mike, he said the dream had something to do with the chaos in my life.

"The rough waters and crashing waves are symbolic of how you feel about your life," he said. He was researching dream analogies on his cellphone.

"And what about the dead guy?" I asked.

He referred to his phone once again. "A dead body," he read. "It represents regret." He gave me a hard look, adding, "A broken relationship. A need for change."

§

My bedroom door opens, breaking my thoughts. "Issy..." My mother enters with a sullen look on her face, and my heart jumps.

"What's wrong?"

"Your father has to go back home for a few days." She sits on the edge of the bed. "A close friend passed away."

"Who?"

I sit up and she lowers her gaze from mine. "No one you know. But..." Her eyes swell with tears as she explains, "We've booked flights. We're leaving this morning." She blinks the tears away. "You'll be okay?"

I nod. "Of course. Don't worry about me."

A gentle smile appears on her weary face and, as she rises to go, I ask, "Is dad okay?"

My mother stops in the middle of the room. She

hesitates. "He'll be okay."

After my parents leave, I pace through the house with Tom, the cat, at my heels. My parents named the cat. "Tom. Real original," I'd told them. My grandfather laughed saying they'd named the cat after him. "Thomas, the Second," he teased.

Sipping on a mug of warm tea, I move from the kitchen to the living room while I contemplate what I'm going to do about my brother. One thing is for damn sure, this time, I won't keep it to myself.

Last night, I received a call from Matt, but I refused to answer. I was still angry with him, and with Ben too. Then, Eric texted me.

'*Matt told me what happened,*" he wrote. '*You need to stop worrying so much. You're going to give yourself an aneurysm.*'

I didn't respond, so Eric sent me another set of texts. '*Everything's fine,*' he stated, '*Promise.*'

Now, tired and anxious, I pace when I notice Tom lying outside of my mother's workroom on a piece of paper. Nearing, I notice that what he's lying on is a photograph.

"Where did you get this?" I ask as though I might get an answer.

Tom and I fight over the photo until he finally relinquishes it to me. Flipping it over, I see that it's the photograph that Eric found in our father's office years ago, the one of my father standing with his arm around a boxer's shoulders. Behind them, the sign on the wall reads, '*The East Side Boys Fight Club.*'

§

During our final year of high school, my brother had grown more rebellious than usual. At the time, he had two fractured ribs and nine stitches in his head, the result of another one of his impromptu fights. As a result, Eric was home from school which was a problem because my brother had a talent for getting himself into trouble.

One day, I came home to find him scrambling through the kitchen cupboards looking for the letter opener.

"What are you doing?" I asked.

"Don't worry about it."

Once he had it in his hand, he set off to pick at the lock to our father's office door.

When Eric heard the click of the lock, he smiled. Apparently, it wasn't the first that he had broken into our father's office, however, it was the first time that I knew about it.

"He's going to kill you," I warned.

"Good. He can put me out of my misery." He entered the office, stepped behind the large oak desk, opened the bottom drawer, and began to rummage through it.

"What are you doing?" I asked, afraid to go beyond the doorway.

"There's something in here."

"What?"

Eric ignored me and continued to shuffle through the drawer. I looked up at the clock on the wall. It was nearing six o'clock and soon our father would come walking through the front door to find us prying through his desk. The idea terrified me.

No longer able to handle the anxiety of the situation, I ran into the room and shoved my brother away from the desk.

"He's seriously going to hurt you."

"I don't care," he snapped back.

"What could you possibly want from here?"

Eric pushed me aside and continued to dig through the drawer, lifting papers and paper clips and pens. "Come on," he grumbled.

I glanced at the clock once again. The panic was overwhelming.

Suddenly, a grin appeared on my brother's face. What Eric discovered was the photo of our father with the boxer. The man's name was Patrick. As children, we called him, Uncle Patrick. Turned out that he wasn't our uncle after all.

"What are you two doing in here?" The rumble of my father's voice sent a chill through me. I was instantly standing at attention, wide-eyed, and frightened. My brother, however, crossed the room and shoved the photo in our father's face.

"You are such a hypocrite," he said.

My father tore the photo from Eric's grasp. He examined it for two seconds, then stormed across the room, and set it back into its rightful place.

Eric went after him. "You're always on me about fighting, and school, and finding a nice quiet desk job. Meanwhile, you were involved in some kind of fight club?" He spat the words out as though in disgust.

"What the hell is that all about?"

"This was a long time ago."

"So, what?"

"So, I'm not this person anymore."

"But it's who you used to be."

My father, already furious, told us to get out of his office but Eric refused.

"Of course," my brother hissed. "Do as I say and not as I do, right?"

"Yes." My father's tone was forceful. "Now, get out."

"Can you at least tell me what happened to Uncle Patrick?"

"He's not your uncle."

"Sure, he is. He came to stay with us -"

"No, he didn't."

"But I remember -"

"No, you don't." Our father ushered us out of his office with a shove. It was then that Eric blew up.

For years, there had been a growing bubble of tension between them. Like an overinflated balloon that could no longer contain the pressure against its thin walls, it now threatened to burst.

"Why can't you just tell me the truth?" Eric shouted out without any thought to consequence. "Why are you always lying to us?"

Our father face turned red and his eyes went white. "Get out."

We left the room then. When our mother also refused to talk about Patrick, Eric and I became suspicious. We couldn't understand the reason for the secrecy. What could they possibly be hiding? Yet, all these years later, my brother and I never forgot about that photo nor the man in the boxing gloves.

Herein lies Pandora's tainted clay jar of deception and lies, ready to be cracked wide open by the unrelenting curiosity of twin minds.

§

The cat enters my mother's workroom, and I follow him in. The door has been left wide open, and papers are scattered across every surface. The disarray is as odd as the unlocked door to my father's office.

Tom jumps onto the cabinet, then dives headfirst into an open drawer. I pull him out before he can get himself lodged in there. As I do, his claws catch on a manila folder, and a photograph slips out. I set the cat down and pick up the photo.

It's another picture of Patrick, except now he's in our kitchen. With his strawberry-blond hair and gentle blue eyes, he stands between my mother and Aunt Rachel. Dressed in simple blue jeans and a dark t-shirt, his arms around the women, he looks like he belongs in one of those old cigar ads. "A man's man," the ad would read.

Then, I notice a second photograph stuck to the back of this one. Cautiously, I pry it free. In the second photo, Patrick sits together with my mother and Rachel on a sofa that I don't recognize, in a room I've never seen before. Eric and I sit over their laps with smiles on our faces.

Looking for a description or a year, I flip the

photograph over. The ink has faded over time, but I can make out a date: November 1996. There's a note too.

'Dear Sara, *I'm so thankful that I got to spend these last four weeks with you and the children. For so long, it's all I've ever wanted. Just some time.*

I wish so much that you didn't have to go. I wish I could make you stay. I wish we could be a family. But I guess this is how it has to be. Perhaps this is punishment for all the wrong I've done in my life.

Just know that I will never stop loving you. Please remember that. And take good care of our babies. I will never forget them – don't let them forget me.

All my love, Patrick'

My heart's pounding. It can't be. Frantic with anticipation, I jump into my small Civic and head to my grandparents' house.

My grandmother answers the front door and instantly, her smile fades into a frown. "Issy. What's wrong?"

I raise the picture of my mother sitting close to Patrick while my brother and I smile gleefully in their arms. Then, I turn the photograph over.

"What does this mean?" I ask.

As her eyes graze across the handwriting on the back, her brow gathers. "Issy, where did you get this?"

In the boredom of a beige folder. *What does it matter?* "Please, tell me it's not true."

With a sigh, my grandmother takes the photograph from me. I'm waiting for her to say, "It's okay. It's not what you think," but she doesn't. Instead, she tells me,

"You weren't supposed to find this."

Gaping back at her, I burst into a sob. "What the hell?"

CHAPTER 14   July 1990

Two months after Patrick took off, I'm invited back to the Sherman home. I wasn't looking forward to facing the devil-woman again, but it was Sara's birthday, and what kind of a friend would I be if I didn't make an appearance?

Standing at the front door, I look down at the gift bag one more time. I picked out the most mature looking one that I could find. The woman at the gift shop stuffed some pink tinsel paper into the bag and fluffed it up like they do at the mall.

With a sigh and surmounting hesitation, I ring the doorbell. It's okay, I give myself a quick pep talk. It's only a couple of hours and Rachel will be here too, so

I'll have plenty of backup.

"David."

It's Thomas, good ol' Tom. I shake the man's hand and enter. "She's out on the deck," he tells me before I can ask. "And look out for the decorations. Laura will have your head if you mess anything up."

The house is decorated in black and white and pink. Over the dining room table, there's a cluster of balloons, and along the living room wall, a large birthday banner is displayed. Confetti sprinkles are scattered throughout the room. They're on the sofa and the table and the floor. There's even some creeping up the stairs – I mean, this shit is everywhere.

Stepping onto the patio deck, I smile. Sara's wrapped in a blanket and reading one of her lengthy novels.

"David." She rises from the large wooden chair. "You came."

Wearing a pair of snug black silky pants and a light pink t-shirt, she approaches me with a hug. "I thought you might not come."

"Why would you say that?"

"Because my mother wants to eat you alive."

I smirk and hand her the gift bag. "Well, I hope your mother doesn't give me shit for this."

Pulling the bottle of rosé from the bag, she gasps with exaggeration. "How did you know?"

"Lucky guess. Figure we can have it later."

"Drink our worries away?" she suggests.

"Something like that."

Setting the bottle on the table, she says, "Well, I'm

nineteen now, and my mother doesn't have a say in what I do or..." she slides her arm through mine, "Who I befriend."

"I'm happy to hear it." I can't stop smiling.

"Come." She pulls me along, down the stairs of the deck, past the grass, and onto the sand.

"Where are we going?"

"For a walk."

"What about your party? Isn't your mother going to get upset if you leave?"

"Oh, come on. Don't be a chicken."

"Right," I laugh. "A chicken." I'd never been accused of that before.

Then, with her sweet smile, she says, "It's a beautiful day. You won't regret it, I promise."

I was all in, and certain that no good could come of this.

For several minutes, we walk together in silence, keeping a safe distance from the tide as it breaks against the shore. I stuff my hands into the pockets of my slack while Sara, both hands holding my arm, leans in a little closer.

She's right. The serenity of the beach, the company, it's all very beautiful. I'd never experienced this kind of peace before. Then again, I'd never met a woman like Sara before. She makes me feel at ease. With her, there is no anger, no agitation, no haunting thoughts of the past. With her, there is only peace and joy, and the fact that she makes me feel anything at all, is exceptional.

"Do you think Patrick's okay?" Her voice is quiet, so

much so that I almost don't hear her. When I ask her to repeat the question, her eyes fill with tears, so I lie.

"I think so."

She looks at me for a moment, as though analyzing my face – *is she as good at detecting lies as her mother?*

"Have you heard from him?"

"No."

"Not even a letter?"

I shake my head and dig my hands deeper into my pockets. "Sorry. Nothing."

It's another lie. Four days ago, I received a phone call from Patrick, but the message that he left on my machine was impossible to comprehend. He said that he was halfway across the country, but he didn't say where. He said that Devons was gone, but did he mean dead and gone or just gone away? It was all left to speculation.

Nothing in Patrick's message was concrete, except for one thing. "Tell Sara I miss her," he said. "Tell her I'm sorry. Make her understand."

How could I possibly make her understand Patrick's reason for leaving when I couldn't make sense of it myself? And what was I to say? That Patrick called and he misses you, but I can't tell you anything else? Why complicate an already complicated situation?

A sudden gust of wind sweeps the grains of sand into the air. Sara hurries to cover her face and I pull her to me and shut my eyes until the wind dies down again.

"Are you alright?" I ask.

"Yeah. That happens sometimes." She begins to smooth her hair back into place with the palms of her hands.

"Here." I adjust a couple of strands of her hair. "All better."

She looks up at me with a tilt of her head. "Why are you so good to me?"

"Am I?" No one had ever said that to me before either.

"Yes. Ever since Patrick left, you've been... different. Kind. Present."

"Maybe it's guilt."

"Guilt?"

I felt guilty for so many things. "Or maybe..." Sara's gaze remains fixed onto mine, waiting for me to elaborate, while I wonder if now is too soon to kiss her. "Maybe, it's because I think you're worth it."

Her smile widens. "I think you're worth it too."

Even though it shouldn't have, her words sting. "I'm really not," I tell her. I'm not worthy of a girl like Sara.

"Of course, you are. The way you care about Patrick. The way you've helped him. Maybe it's not who you used to be but it's who you've become."

I think about it for a minute, wondering if she's right. I'm not the same person that I used to be. I'd left that guy way back on the other side of the ocean. Here, I'm someone else, someone new.

Looking down at her bright brown eyes and her dark hair blowing in the breeze, I want nothing more than to take her face into the palms of my hands and kiss her. But I don't. Instead, I offer her my arm once more, and we walk back to the house in silence.

Entering through the patio doors, I notice Laura's

eyes on us. Seated on the sofa with her friend, Laura watches us – watches me: the smile on my face, my casual ease with her daughter.

There was nothing the devil-woman could say or do to bring me down.

Seated on my grandparent's sofa, I struggle to catch my breath.

I remember when Patrick came to visit. I can also still recall his Irish accent, although, at four years of age, my exact words were "weird accent." My mother scolded me when I said it out loud, but Patrick didn't mind. He laughed, picked me up, and spun me around. Eric and I took to him instantly. Mostly, I remember how my mother smiled. I'd never known her to be so happy. But then, something happened. Patrick left and we never saw him again.

"Issy..." My grandmother breaks my numbing thoughts and I return my gaze to the photograph on my lap.

"Does my father know?" I ask. "Does he know that we're not his?"

"Yes."

"And Patrick?" I choke back tears. "Did he know then that we belong to him?"

"Yes." She points to the photo. "When he returned, he learned of it then."

I'm overcome with emotion. He knew. He knew, and he left us anyway.

"Issy, honey..." My grandmother reaches out to me and wipes away the tears. "Patrick didn't leave you because he wanted to."

"Why then?"

A soft sigh escapes her. "The first time he left it was due to a job offer out west. Or, at least, that's the story your father told. Truth of it is, there was a break-in at the apartment, and it landed Patrick in the hospital."

"He was attacked?"

"Yes, quite badly is my understanding. Three days later, he vanished. Poof." She waves her hand in the air. "Just like that. David wouldn't admit that Patrick's disappearance had anything to do with that break-in but, Patrick ceased all communications. He wouldn't have done that under normal circumstances." She looks outside, through the sliding door, and out to the lake. "Your mother was devastated. She cried for a week straight."

I shake my head in disbelief. "And what happened the second time?"

A weary look comes over my grandmother's face, "It

was just time to leave."

I hold up the photo of Patrick in our kitchen, "Was this the last time he was here?"

She takes the picture into her hands. "I believe so. He arrived just in time for your birthday."

"He knew it was our birthday?"

"I don't know."

"Why didn't he stay in touch?"

"I don't know."

"Did he try to reach out to us?"

"Issy, honey, I truly don't know. You'd have to ask your mother but..." She hesitates before adding. "She doesn't like to speak of those days."

I know that much, although, my mother once told me a story about a boyfriend. She called him, John. This was long before my father came along, she said. She was madly in love with John but one day he left, and she was heartbroken. I remember her eyes glossing over with tears when she spoke of him. Of course, I now understand that story to be about Patrick.

Except, now that I think about it, I'm realizing that this story has a large gap, a five-year gap in fact, between Patrick's initial departure and his return meaning... "He must have returned somewhere in between."

My grandmother raises her eyebrows in thought saying, "No doubt. We knew that she was pregnant before she married. But, of course, the assumption was that you and Eric belonged to David. There was no reason to think otherwise. What I do know is that once Patrick left, your parents began spending way too much time together. And when they announced their engagement, I was just as surprised as anyone because it was clear to me that your mother wasn't over Patrick."

"Then why did she do it? If she was still so in love with Patrick, why did she marry my father?"

She shrugs. "Love. Convenience."

Yanking the photo from her hand, I glare at Patrick's smiling face and toss the picture onto the living room table. "They should have told us."

"I'm sure your parents only wanted to protect you."

"Protect me from what?"

"The pain of his absence, I suppose."

"I can understand that they would want to protect us as children but we're not children anymore and we have a right to know." My voice rises in frustration. "Were they ever going to tell us the truth? Or were they just going to carry on pretending that David is our father."

My grandmother turns to me with anger on her face. "David may have his flaws, but he is your father."

"But he's not, is he? He just happens to be the guy that my mother married to cover up her pregnancy."

"Isabella," her tone is stern now. "He's been nothing if not loyal to you and your mother." I lean back in the seat and lower my head. "And never once did he complain or refrain from his duties as a father. Your entire lives, he's been by your side. Don't you forget that." My grandmother's gaze turns towards the table where all three photos now lie. "And he did it despite what I thought of him."

I look at her, my curiosity growing.

"I wasn't very kind to him," she explains. "Truth of it

is, I couldn't stand the man." She flashes me a sideways glance. "I mean, I really couldn't stand him."

"Why not?" I feel an automatic inclination to protect my father.

"There was something about him," she says. "He was much too confident for his own good."

I can't help the half-smile that comes over me. "He sounds just like Eric."

"Very true," she says. "I told your grandfather that the man reminded me of a snake charmer." She laughs. "But your grandfather liked David just fine. He didn't think anything wrong of him. But..." Her eyes narrow as though rummaging through the memories in her mind. "When I saw him standing in my living room with that fresh haircut and shave and the new preppy shirt, I knew he was trying to bedazzle everyone with his shiny exterior. Everyone found him quite charming, of course. Your father has that way with people, but I saw right through him. I knew he was hiding something."

"Hiding what?"

"I don't know, something. Point is, I didn't like it."

"Because he was a snake charmer," I tease.

"Yes, there's that," she says with a smirk. "And he was already too old for your mother."

"They're only a few years apart."

"Sure, now it doesn't seem like a big deal but, back then you're mother had just turned nineteen and David was pushing twenty-five."

I wrinkle my nose at the thought.

"Naturally, I figured he was just looking to put another notch on his belt."

I cringe. There's an image I don't need in my head.

"Anyhow," my grandmother waves her hand in front of my face as though to dust away the idea that she'd just planted there. "I told your mother he was no good, but she refused to listen. I told her that I didn't want her seeing him, but it only made her want him more. So, I tried to appeal to him. I said, aren't there enough women in all of the GTA to keep you busy?"

"Oh, God." I cover my ears. "Please, stop."

My grandmother forces my arms down. "Point is, he could have kicked me out of the apartment right then and there, and I'm certain that he wanted to, but he didn't."

"Wait, you went to his apartment?"

She nods. "Sure did. I marched over there and told him exactly what I thought of him."

I grimace. My grandmother, now into her early sixties, had recently taken up jogging and weightlifting. She looks as hot as she did in her forties. As strong and confident as she is, I'm not surprised that she might do something like that.

"It was early in the morning on a Sunday when I knocked on his door," she says. "He opened up wearing nothing but a pair of grey pyjama pants. I looked him up and down, and I can still remember that cocky smirk on his face. He thought I was checking him out. Imagine that." She laughs out loud. "I wasn't intrigued by him or his physique. What I was thinking was that he probably had a housekeeper, and I couldn't help but wonder if she did more for him than just clean his apartment."

I shut my eyes tight as if to block out the thought of my father getting it on with his cleaning lady.

"So, I pointed a finger right in his face," she says, "And I told him, I don't want you seeing my daughter. And do you know what that little bastard said to me?"

I open my eyes and shake my head, eager to make her stop.

"He told me to go to hell."

Chapter 16   September 1990

I couldn't understand why the devil-woman was standing in my living room, but there she was, arms crossed, ponytail bopping, and eyes grazing the grooves of my bare chest.

"What can I do for you, Laura?"

She turns towards the living room. "You have a housekeeper."

"Yes." *What is it with this woman?* "Is there something I can do for you?"

She faces me once again and, with her usual bland expression, she says, "I want you to stop seeing my daughter."

Looking down at the woman, I want nothing more than to tell her to go to hell, but I can't. This is Sara's mother and our relationship, if it is to progress, depends on Tom and Laura's acceptance, whether I like it or not.

I take a deep breath. "You know I'm not going to do that."

"Why not?"

"Because I care about her too much."

"Oh, come on, David. A good-looking guy like you, a man of your calibre, don't tell me that there aren't enough women around to keep you busy?"

I can't help but laugh at the comment. Was she insulting me or boosting my ego? "Is that what you're worried about? That I might have a harem?"

"Sara is young," she says. "She has her whole life ahead of her."

Holding my front door wide open, I ask, "What exactly do you mean?"

"I mean that I don't want you to ruin her."

"Ruin her?" With all attempts at composure now dissipated, I tell her, "Look, I don't know who you think I am -"

"I know exactly who you are," she says. Then, with a stout upper lip, her face stiffer than ever, she proceeds to tell me exactly who I am. "You've struggled your whole life. You probably found yourself in a heap of trouble now and then and, over the years, you've learned how to get by on your wit and your charm. But, somewhere along the way, you decided that it was more beneficial and lucrative to go against the rules than to follow them." The corner of her mouth rises. "Am I warm?"

"You've got me all figured out, don't you?" Releasing the door, I take a step towards her, and the door closes behind me. "Tell me, Laura, why is it that you can't stand me?" She makes no attempt to answer and I sneer in response. "That's okay, because I have a theory."

She stares up at me, her lips pressed and her arms still crossed.

"I think you don't like me because you can't figure me out. Because you can't understand how someone like me can come here, find a decent job, excel at it, and manage to get the girl too."

Laura's expression doesn't falter. "I think you're full of shit, that's what I think."

Unbelievable, even when she's insulting me, the woman remains fully composed. She's as smooth as ice on a walkway, just waiting for the thwack of my head to hit the ground.

"You tell people lies," she presses on. "You tell them whatever they want to hear like this story about Patrick running off for a new job opportunity. I know there's more to it. Just like I know that there's more to your reason for leaving England." She lowers her arms and the keys to her Mercedes jingle in her hand. "Which is why I don't want you around my daughter. I don't want Sara caught up in whatever the hell you've got going on."

My jaw tenses and the muscles in my arms stiffen. If she were anyone else...

"What happened, David?" She continues to test me. "Why did you really leave home?"

It's the first time that anyone has ever called me out like this. I don't know how to respond. So, I turn around, open the door to the apartment, and tell her to get out.

A grin emerges over Laura's face. "I get it," she says as she saunters towards the open door. "You were looking for a clean slate and I respect that. But, you see, David..." Out in the hallway, she turns to face me. "Guys like you don't stay clean for long. Sooner or later, you'll make a mistake and, when you do, Sara will leave you."

The woman had struck a nerve. Unable to contain my anger, I tell her to "Go to hell," and slam the door shut.

The confrontation had left me shaken. What the hell is this woman's problem? I'm not good enough for her daughter, she'd made that clear from the start. Now, she thinks that she can come into my home and make demands. The woman's got some set of balls on her, I'll give her that much.

"You're a sadistic son of a bitch," Patrick had once told me. "That's why she doesn't like you. She can see right through you."

Easy for him to say, Laura liked Patrick just fine. He was fit for her daughter but me, oh no, not me.

But... what if she's right? What if I'm not good enough?

"Bitch." I charge across the room, my blood boiling. "God damn, bitch." Without thought, I put my fist through the wall. "Shit."

The door to the bedroom swings opens. "David." Sara's standing in a tank top and underwear, just as I'd left her.

"It's okay," I tell her.

She takes my hand and examines the fresh scrapes

on my knuckles.

"It's fine." I pull away. "I'm fine."

"She had no right to say those things to you." She takes hold of my hand again and, again, I pull away.

"Sara, stop."

"Why?"

I can't bring myself to look at her. "She's right about me."

"What are you talking about?"

The entire time that Laura was piecing my life together, making accusations, and plotting my demise, I'd come to an unfortunate conclusion of my own. If there was any hope of removing Sara from the chaos of my life, I was going to have to do it now.

"You're better off without me," I tell her.

"What? No." Her hands are on my arms, forcing me closer.

"Sara. Please."

"Why are you letting her get to you?"

"You deserve better than this - better than me."

"I don't care about the past - whatever you did - whatever happened, it doesn't matter anymore." Tears fill her eyes and it makes my heart ache. "I care about you," she cries out. "I love you."

She kisses me hard on the lips.

"Sara..."

"Please, David, don't do this."

I look down into her tear-filled eyes. I can't give her up - I won't give her up. Unable to resist her any longer, I take her into my arms and kiss her. In that instant, I made a decision that I'll never be able to take back. But

I also know that I've never felt this way for any woman before.

Sara's breaths hasten, matching my own, and I lift her into my arms. With her legs wrapped around my waist, my lips on hers, I carry her back to bed.

'Things fall apart; the centre cannot hold;
Mere anarchy is loosed upon the world,
The blood-dimmed tide is loosed, and
everywhere, The ceremony of innocence
is drowned'

Some poems speak to you, others explain your life in its entirety. When I was four years old, I watched my father beat a man unconscious in our backyard. Seated at the kitchen table with Eric one morning, we watched our father as he stormed across the room. The rumble of his voice echoed through the walls. Out on the deck, he fought the man, Patrick.

My parents refused to speak of the incident. Anytime that my brother and I brought up Patrick's name, they diverted the conversation. It was as though Patrick only existed in our memories or in those old photographs.

My cellphone buzzes. It's on the kitchen counter right under Tom, and the vibration sends the cat running. Standing in front of the French doors, I look down at the screen. It's Adrian.

All the way home from my grandparent's house, I'd tried to reach him. First, I called Eric. I needed to tell him what I'd discovered about our father, our real father. When he didn't answer, I called Victoria, but she didn't pick up either. So, I called Adrian. His phone went straight to voice mail. In the past, I would have called Mike.

"Hey," I answer and Adrian cuts me off. He's rambling frantically.

"Hold on," I tell him. "Slow down."

"He broke it off, Issy. Sam broke it off."

My heart sinks. "No. Why?"

"Can I come over?"

"Of course."

Twenty minutes later, Adrian is slumped over my parents' couch with his knees apart and one hand to his mouth. He sits in that pose for a long while, as though in disbelief.

"What did he say?" I ask.

"Apparently, I don't know what I want."

I frown, certain that he must be mistaken. "Perhaps

it was a misunderstanding."

"He says I'm more involved with my friends than with him."

"He sounds like Mike."

"Yeah, turns out they're both nuts."

We fall silent, the two of us staring ahead at nothing, until Adrian says, "It was the first time I'd actually felt something real, you know?" His eyes begin to glisten.

I don't know what to say. I've never seen this side of Adrian before, the side that isn't hiding behind playful jokes and a charming smile. I didn't know that it existed. But I imagine that this is Adrian in the raw, that part of him that he doesn't want other people to know about.

"Do you have any liquor?" he asks.

I turn to him, surprised by the request. "Well, yes, in my father's office but -"

"Good." He gets up and goes into the office, no longer under lock and key, and soon re-emerges with a bottle of whiskey. "Come on," he says, heading towards the kitchen.

My father's going to kill me. Except that he's not my father so, maybe it doesn't matter.

Out on the deck, Adrian takes back a shot of whiskey. He pours himself a second drink and slides onto the deck chair. Then, just as quickly, he shifts forward again as though he's about to get up and leave.

"Damn it." He takes back the shot. "I screwed up, Issy."

"Talk to him. Try to work things out."

He shakes his head at me. "He said he's done."

Fresh tears rise into his eyes. "Thing is, I'm afraid I'll never feel that way again, you know?"

I reach out to him and squeeze his hand. "You will."

Adrian smiles and wipes the dampness from his cheeks. Then, as he reaches for the bottle of whiskey left on the arm of the chair, it slips from his fingers and splatters onto his t-shirt and jeans.

"Damn it." He jumps to his feet, slapping the remnants of liquor from his lap.

Rushing into the laundry room, we rinse off the stains under hot water and toss the clothes into the wash. Adrian is left standing in nothing more than a pair of snug black Calvin Klein boxers. Luckily, Adrian's incredibly comfortable with his nakedness. I, on the other hand, can hardly stand to be in my own skin.

Looking down at himself, Adrian mutters, "Damn, I'm a mess."

"Well, at least you're a hot mess."

Adrian looks at me, and we burst into laughter.

In the kitchen, I brew coffee while Adrian insists that he doesn't want any.

"Yes, you do." I've been through this too many times. "And you'll thank me for it later."

He doesn't argue further. Instead, he sits at the kitchen table where the three pictures of Patrick are sprawled out.

"Who's this guy?" he asks, holding the photo of Patrick standing in our kitchen with my mother and Rachel.

"My father," I tell him as a matter of fact.

Amused, he turns to me with a grimace. "What do you mean?"

"That man is my real father."

Adrian's grin fades. "Issy..." He gets up and comes to stand in front of me. "Are you serious?"

I explain how I found the photographs earlier that day. "They were hidden in my mother's workroom." I tell him about the picture on the floor, the cat in the drawer, the revelation at my grandmother's house, followed by her admittance of the truth.

"Except for this one." I take hold of the photo of Patrick with my father's arm around him – David's arm. "Eric and I already knew about this one." There was nothing odd or peculiar about this photo, except for the fact that my father was involved in some sort of illegal fighting ring.

"Damn, Issy, this is nuts. You do know that, right?"

"I know."

"I mean..." He returns his focus to the photographs. "It's absurd."

"What's absurd is that my mother had an affair with Patrick."

"How do you know?"

I did the math; there's no way around it. "The only way that Eric and I can be his is if my mother was with Patrick during the winter of 1992. By then, my parents were already engaged."

My heart hurts to think of it. My father is the toughest man I know, except when it comes to his children, and my mother.

"Shit. Does Eric know?"

I shake my head. "I don't think so."

This was my parent's big secret, I come to realize, the thing that they had tried so hard to keep from us. Now, it had been blown wide open.

"How's my favourite investor?" the sultry voice calls out.

Rachel is standing by the back wall of the shop wearing a mauve jacket that matches the swatches of patterns in her hands.

"I'm good," I tell her. "How's my favourite interior decorator?"

She sets the fabrics down on the counter. "The same as usual," she says. "You know, demands, complaints, more demands." Standing in front of me, Rachel looks over her shoulder as though someone might be there then, holds out her hand. "Give me a puff of your cigarette."

I'm not holding a cigarette. In fact, I had just butted one out. Regardless, I do as she requests. Stepping out onto the snowy sidewalk, I light up another one and hand it to her.

"No, just a puff," she hisses.

"Alright." I light one for myself anyway knowing damn well that she isn't going to take just one puff.

With a sigh, Rachel blows the smoke out slowly.

"I don't know why you keep doing this to yourself," I tell her. "Just buy a pack already."

"I told you. Frank's constantly on my ass about it. Imagine if he found a pack on me."

This, I find amusing. As if a woman like Rachel cared about what anyone thought of her, including her husband. "So, keep it in the shop," I suggest and, instantly, I'm met by the woman's fierce glare.

"Now, why the hell didn't I think of that? Oh yeah, because I'd still smell like a chimney."

I laugh. The woman's feisty, like a firecracker, and she's sharp too. But what I like most about Rachel is that she doesn't take shit from anyone.

"So..." I begin, somewhat hesitant, "I bought a house today."

Rachel's gaze widens. "You bought a house?"

With one hand in my coat pocket, I lower my head and take a long drag of my cigarette. "I did."

Typically, I would be eager to share big news like this but, this isn't about gains or accomplishments. Today, it's about a potential rejection that might very well impact me at a level I'd never felt before.

The house, an old Colonial two-story build, is situated along the lakeshore not far from the Shermans' home. It came up for grabs when the seller was forced to liquify his assets. I'd been told it had something to do with the rippling effects of the economic crash in '87. Those effects were still trickling into the nineties. I jumped at the opportunity.

"That's wonderful." Rachel throws her arms around me. "First the engagement, now this."

A bashful smile comes over me. On New Year's Eve, I proposed. It was a bit cliché, I know, but I wanted to start the new year right. It was a big deal for someone like me. I was certain that marriage wasn't meant for me, but Sara said "Yes" and, from that moment on, my life was different. I was different.

This house, it meant everything, because more improbable than marriage was the idea that I might be worthy of a family. The thought consumed me. Ever since it crept into my mind, it had taken hold of my every waking moment. Me, a father? I was nervous as hell.

But bashful? I wasn't bashful - that wasn't me.

"Well, tell me about this house," Rachel says.

"It's a two-story red-brick. Built in the 1950s." Two tall white columns rise from the first step up to the rooftop. A proper house, I'd thought, built for a proper family.

"Sounds amazing."

"It is. And the staircase, you should see it. It's incredible." I was told that the circular staircase with the decorative bannister is original cherry wood. "You don't see that anymore."

"No," she agrees. "You don't."

"And I'll have my own office at the front of the house." The office, situated to the right of the living room, is aligned with wall-to-wall bookshelves and two large windows.

"That's great. You'll keep out of Sara's hair then," she says with a chuckle.

I laugh. "Yes, I suppose so. But I imagine we'll be spending most of our time in the yard."

"The yard?"

Through a set of French doors, the patio overlooks half an acre of lush green landscape with a thick leafy forest as a backdrop. Sara would say it's enchanting.

Rachel smiles at me. "Are you blushing, Mr. Bauer?"

I scoff and lower my gaze from hers. "I don't blush." Then, taking a final puff of the cigarette, I say, "I'd like Sara to see it this afternoon. Would you mind sparing her for an hour or so?"

"Wait -" Rachel squints as the smoke rises past her face. "Weren't you with her?"

The dread is immediate. She doesn't have to say another word. The suspicion is already there.

"She got a call," Rachel says with some confusion. "Ran out of here like a banshee in heat. I figured she was with you."

Throwing the cigarette to the ground, I mutter a hard, "No."

"Oh..."

What else could she say?

"And you don't know where she is?" It was more of a statement than a question that Rachel then confirms with a slow shake of her head.

There was no reason to suspect Sara of being deceptive nor unfaithful. She'd never given me a reason to feel this way and yet, the feeling was there.

Much later that night, Sara pulls into her parent's driveway. Seated in my car, I watch as she parks her vehicle next to mine and, with the porch light shining onto her face, she turns to look at me. Her eyes are swollen, as though she's been crying.

I reach over and open the passenger door from the inside. Sara enters, but she won't meet my gaze.

All evening I've been mulling over the possibilities. There was no explanation for her sudden erratic behaviour except for one thing or, rather, one person.

"Where have you been?" I ask.

She hesitates longer than she should. "I was in the city."

"Why?"

Again, there's a long pause. Why is she making this so damn hard?

"I got a call today," she says.

"From who?" I have a terrible feeling that I already know. Six months of silence, why now?

Her voice is a mere whisper as she says his name, "Patrick."

"He called you?"

She looks at me and I can see the sadness in her eyes. "He wanted to see you too, but..." She doesn't finish the sentence and, somehow, it doesn't matter.

"Where did you meet him?"

"I told you -"

"Where, Sara?" I didn't mean to shout. I was trying to remain calm, to give her the benefit of the doubt, but it was proving harder than I thought.

Near tears, she tells me that they met in a hotel.

I turn away, my mind swirling with the obvious but refusing to accept it. "What happened?"

She doesn't answer.

"Sara." I grab her by the arm. "Tell me what the hell happened."

She shakes her head while tears drip down her cheeks. "Nothing..."

"Clearly, it's something." I release her. "Or else you wouldn't have that look on your face."

She rubs her thumb over the engagement ring, and my first instinct is to hit the dashboard – release the rage. Instead, I shut my eyes and try to be reasonable. She wasn't over Patrick when she came to me. I know that. But I presumed that she was over him once she had opened herself up to me, accepted me, and my proposal. I'm such a fool.

"Patrick never wrote to me," she says suddenly.

I open my eyes. In the palm of her hand lies the engagement ring alongside a tiny square piece of paper.

"He never wrote that letter." She closes her hand into a fist. "Why did you do it?"

It's true. Patrick didn't write her that letter. I did, but I had my reasons for doing it. "I wanted to protect you. To make it hurt less."

"No, you wanted me to think that he'd left for good, didn't you?"

"What? That's absurd."

"So, you could have me to yourself."

"Really? This is on me now?" I can't help the

scathing bite on my tongue. "Because I don't remember you resisting."

Sara holds her hand open, once again revealing the ring and paper. "I can live with a lot of crap, David. But I can't live with the constant lies."

Without a word, I take the ring and the damn paper and Sara rushes out of the car and into her parent's house. I'm such an idiot for falling in love. What the hell was I thinking?

Seated in the parking lot of the apartment building, I pull the items from my pocket. Holding the ring in my fist, I unfold the small square piece of paper. It has been folded and refolded several times over, as though its owner had been agitated or nervous.

'David,

I want you to know that there are no hard feelings on my end. I never expected Sara to wait for me and I'm happy for the two of you. I really am. If anyone is capable of watching out for her, it's you. But you need to know that I love her more than anything in this world, and I will always love her.'

So far, the ink of the pen was sketched hard into the note. But, the next part of Patrick's message is smoother and less jagged.

'I don't know if they're onto me or not, but I can't sit around waiting. I'm going overseas for a while, and I don't know when, or if I can return. And mate, you've always been

*like a brother to me. I don't blame you for any of this. I want
you to know that. Take care of yourself and take care of Sara.*
Your best mate, Patrick'

Gripping the steering wheel, I rest my forehead against my knuckles. I wish it had been me to pull that trigger back at Barton's estate and not Patrick. I would have done the job right the first time around and, when they'd come looking for me, I'd have gladly handed myself in. I wouldn't run. I'd stopped running.

Besides, I would have nothing to run from. Sara would still be with Patrick, and I would never know just how happy she can make me. At the very least, jail would have ended my misery of wanting a woman I couldn't have. And I'd have bigger problems in prison, anyhow.

Still, I'd rather that than the pain of this heartbreak.

Four weeks, that's how long it took me to cave in and call her. "Sara... can I see you?" I can't help myself.

From the other end of the phone, I hear a brief pause followed by a hushed, "Yes."

Once again parked in front of the lake, I watch as the water crashes into the ice boulders that have formed on the shore.

Focused on the ice ahead, I mutter, "I'm sorry..."

We hadn't said a word to each other since I picked her up. Now, sitting here in the silence of the night, it was time to tell her what was on my mind.

"I'm sorry that I lied about the letter." I'm sorry for so many things. "But you have to believe that I did it with good intentions."

Sara remains silent.

"Look." I turn to face her. "I should tell you to go find someone else."

"David -"

"Just – please, let me talk."

Sara lowers her head, and I take a deep breath. I'm not sure where I'm going with this, but I know I have to get it out. "Maybe you could learn to be happy with someone else, someone who's more like him and less like me. But you see..." An exasperated sigh escapes me. "The problem is that I love you, and I can't convince myself otherwise."

Through a dampened gaze, Sara reaches out to me, and I wrap her into my arms. I didn't understand it. I was a man of certainty, and I'd always made a point of preparing myself for the inevitable. Yet, everything I knew of myself failed when it came to Sara. She continued to challenge me, forcing me to feel things I never thought possible, and behave in ways I'd never imagined.

"David..." Sara's arms wrap around my neck and she leans her face close to mine. "I'm sorry that I hurt you," she whispers. "I thought that being with you would bring me closer to him, but the thing is..." I can feel her tears on my cheek. "When I thought I'd lost you, that's when I realized... I'm so in love with you."

Sara had caused a ripple in my world that I could never escape. I was madly in love and it seemed quite evident that absolutely nothing was going to change that.

The sun is peaking over the ledge of my windowsill as I awaken. On the left side of my double-bed, the sheet is pulled back, and I can still see the indent on the pillow from Adrian's head. We had laid awake late into the night talking, laughing, crying. He was heartbroken and certain that he would never get over it. I assured him that he would. One day, someone would come along and make him feel the way Sam did. But even as I spoke, I thought of Mike and wondered if I believed my own words.

Suddenly struck by the tantalizing aroma of freshly brewed coffee, I jump out of bed, wash up, change, and head downstairs. In the living room, I find Adrian seated on the sofa still wearing nothing but his boxers. In one hand, he holds a mug of coffee and, in the other, he has my photos.

As I ease myself onto the sofa next to him, Adrian forces a grin. "Are you okay?" I ask.

He nods. "I talked to Sam this morning. Well, we texted, but that's okay. At least he spoke to me."

I smile at him. "That's a good start, right?"

He shrugs. "He's still certain that he doesn't want to get back with me but, he says we should act like adults about it. So, that's what I'm doing."

Wouldn't life be simpler if we could just want the same things?

"Anyway," he holds the photo's up to me. "I still can't believe this." He shakes his head. "I mean, to keep it from you for so long, it doesn't make sense."

I agree. It doesn't make sense. "And it's so unlike my mother."

"The secrecy?" he asks.

"No, the cheating."

"Are you sure she had an affair? I mean, maybe the timing's off?"

"I'm certain of it." I'd spent hours thinking through the facts, the timing of events, and the dates. It all adds up. Then, I analyzed the photos: Patrick's arm around my mother, his hand gripping her hip, the smile on her face; it was much too intimate. And who knows how long it went on for. Despite all the facts, it made no sense to me because... "My mother is not this person. She's the kindest, most angelic person I know."

"Well, Issy, no offense but you don't know how she

used to be."

I'm insulted by the insinuation. "What are you saying?"

"I just mean that you only know her as "mom." You don't know what she was like before she became a mother."

Looking back at him through pressed lips, I tell him that if my mother behaved out of the ordinary, it was purely out of love because that's how she is.

"She's a romantic. She follows her heart."

§

My mother had always been very open with us. She told my brother and I of certain events in her childhood with her parents, with Stephen, of the move to Port Credit all those years ago. She'd told us of the miscarriage that my grandmother had at five months. The baby was to be named Marie. My mother was only four years old at the time, but she remembers the sadness in the home during those days.

And there was that story of the boyfriend she once had before my father came along, the one she called, John. That story had aroused a slew of questions from me, which my mother proceeded to answer with her usual patience.

"Did you love him?" I asked.

"Yes."

"What did he look like?"

"Tall, handsome, and the most gentle blue eyes you've ever seen."

I wasn't sure what that meant, but he sounded wonderful. Then came the natural tendency to protect my own interests. "Did you leave him because you fell in love with dad?"

My mother, sitting out on the steps of our deck, smiled. "Yes."

Even at twelve years of age, I sensed that she wasn't being entirely truthful, but I liked the answer and decided not to probe further. In the end, the boyfriend had to go away, and so my mother was forced to move on.

§

"And you never heard from him again?" Adrian asks.

"Patrick? No."

"Why did he leave?"

I lean against the sofa and look up at the shiny crystals hanging off the chandelier. When Patrick was here, he would spin me around in the living room. I'd lean back with my arms spread out and stare up at the brilliance of those crystals and, in that moment, I became a fairy princess in my crystal palace.

As the memories swirl around in my mind, I tell Adrian, "My father fought him."

"Patrick and your father fought?"

I take a deep breath. "Yes." To this day, the thought of my father and Patrick fighting nauseates me. I remember the violence, the blood; it was horrible.

"Do you know what it was about?" he asks.

"No, and my parents refuse to talk about it."

Adrian shakes his head at the absurdity. "What

about her?" He holds up one of the photos with my aunt.

"That's my Aunt Rachel," I tell him.

"Where is she at?"

"Europe."

"Hm." Adrian studies the photo. "Maybe your father found out that he wasn't your biological father."

I'm disturbed by the thought. "He must have known. I mean, he must have married her knowing, right?"

"Maybe not. Maybe that's what provoked the fight." Adrian's eyes focus on mine. "And it's the reason why Patrick left the second time around. Because your mother made a choice."

I can still hear the rumble of my father's voice echoing through the house that day. It terrified me. The fear I felt that day, the panic drawing deep into my bones, it made me want to curl up into the tiniest ball and disappear. At times, I still want to disappear.

Suddenly, there's a knock on the front door. Simultaneously, Adrian and I look to one another.

"Are you expecting someone?" he whispers.

Frantically, I hiss back, "No."

The Keeper of Things

Part III

The knock on the front door is loud and determined to be answered. Seated in my office, I watch the twins' race across the living room, Eric in his bedsheet cape and Issy with her paper roll sword.

"Hey." I jump off the sofa as they run towards the front door, "Do not open that door." But, even as the words leave my lips, I know I'm already too late.

Stepping out of my office, I find the front door pulled wide open. The twins are standing side by side, their little chins raised and their mouths gaping in awe of the giant before them. Now, I too stand in awe. I can't believe it

"David." The large man with the loud voice pats

the twins on their little heads. Then, passing between them, he throws his arms around me and slaps me hard on the back.

"Patrick." I'm stumped. In fact, I'm almost speechless. "Jesus."

"Nope, just me," he says with a chuckle.

Patrick looks exactly the same except, somehow, he seems taller and thicker than I remember. He stops mid-laugh, and I follow his gaze to the centre of the living room where Sara now stands staring back at him.

He moves towards her and envelopes her in a tight embrace. Sara, wide-eyed and bewildered, turns to look at me. If I didn't know better, I'd think she was afraid.

As they pull apart, Patrick asks how's she's been.

"Good," she whispers, trying to compose herself.

Patrick smiles at her. Then, forcing his gaze from hers, he looks down at the children at her side.

"And who do we have here?"

"Eric," the boy shouts out, his bright blue-green eyes wide.

"I'm Issy." She smiles her shy little smile back at him.

"I see." Patrick kneels in front of them and looks them over. "Although, judging by the valiant cape and sword, I say from now on you shall be called Sir Eric and Lady Isabella."

The children laugh and giggle.

"Hm..." Rubbing his fingertips across his chin, he says, "You know what you're missing though?"

"What?" they ask in unison.

"A shield."

They gasp at the mention of it.

"Every great warrior needs a shield," he says. "Lucky for you," Patrick rises and, with his feet apart and his hands on his waist, he stands like he's some kind of superhero. "I happen to be an expert in the shield-making business." The twins' eyes widen in awe once again. They barely know him and they're already in love with the idea of him. "Perhaps, after dinner, I'll make one for each of you."

The children cheer.

"That is…" Patrick looks from me to Sara. "If I'm invited to dinner."

"Of course. Of course, you're invited." Sara and I stumble over our words.

The twins' cheers ring out louder. Then, taking Patrick by the hand, they guide him towards the kitchen. Sara turns to me and I can't help but look at her with the same stunned expression.

After dinner, we head onto the patio. While the children run around the yard with their new shields, Sara and I listen to Patrick's stories of the new life he's made for himself in Europe.

"You said you would write," she says, seated across from him at the picnic table. "You said you would let me know where you've settled."

"Aye, I know. And I meant to."

"You promised."

She's still hurt by his absence - I get it. It was sudden and unexpected. I'm also curious to know where he's been during his five-year hiatus.

"I'm sorry." There's regret on his face. "I had every intention of it..." His voice trails off, and he turns his attention to me. "I've been staying in a place called Cascais. It's a small coastal town in Portugal."

"Wait -" Sara narrows her gaze in thought. "Isn't that where Rachel and Frank have their apartment?"

"It is."

"You've been staying in their apartment?"

In the yard, Issy's giggles ring out, followed by Eric's warrior cries.

"When did this happen?" Sara's tone grows stern.

"It doesn't matter," he says.

Sara presses her lips together and rises. Then, glaring across at Patrick, she states, "It does matter."

As she disappears into the house, Patrick leans his arms against the table and lowers his head. "Should have kept my mouth shut, huh?"

"Hm." I hum in a manner of agreement. I know exactly when it happened. That night – that one damn night.

"It doesn't matter what I tell her," he continues. "She wants the truth, and I can't give it to her."

"Don't worry about it." I gulp my beer. "She'll get over it. How long are you here?"

"Not sure."

"You got a one-way ticket or something?"

The smirk returns to Patrick's face.

"How?"

"How what?"

"You've been gone five years - without a word," I remind him, "So, how are you here now? What changed?"

He reaches into his back pocket and pulls out his wallet. "I didn't know if they were after me."

"They who?"

"The police." He says it as a matter of fact, as though I should know this. "I didn't know if they'd figured me out, but I wasn't going to wait around to find out."

"Figured out what, Patrick?" Not even alcohol can ease the headaches I get when trying to syphon information from this guy.

He stops digging through his wallet, leans towards me, and whispers, "That I'd killed him."

Unbelievable, he's still on this shit. "You're talking about Devons?"

"Of course. Who else would it be?" A deep frown follows the statement. "Shit. You still don't believe me?"

I turn my gaze away and take back another gulp of the ale.

"Damn, had I known it would be this hard to convince you, I'd have brought the man's head as proof."

I can't help the grin that comes over me, and Patrick laughs.

"Here." He hands me his license.

The face is his, but the name reads, 'Nathan Michaels.'

"I met a lady who got me some connections." He shrugs. "So, now I'm this guy."

I look across at him, once again stumped. "Just how many concussions did you get?"

"You're still a bastard." He takes his license from me. "And I'm not fightin' anymore." He taps the card against his temple. "It's like an egg-shell. That's what the doctors tell me, anyway."

Sliding the card back into his wallet, he takes the beer into his hand and says, "I half-believe them, but I'm not stupid to risk it. I cut out the bars and anything else that might bring me joy. Maybe a girl now and then." He finishes with a smile and a chug of his ale.

"Glad it hasn't slowed you down."

"Nah, I'm hittin' the gym like never before. Gotta do something so I don't go mad." Then, he hands me another card. "Also got my business up and running."

This one is a business card that reads, 'Michaels Landscaping.'

"Shit. You've been busy."

"Yup. Even have my eye on a little cottage up in the mountains."

"Really?" This is unexpected, considering I thought he was dead. "I'm happy for you, man."

Patrick nods in acknowledgment and requests another beer. We sit out there drinking and reminiscing until Patrick's almost too drunk to walk.

Sara had come outside once to call the children in for bed. They went willingly, their eyes droopy, and their new shields dragging behind them. Without looking at us, she told us, "Goodnight," and went back inside.

I offered Patrick the pull-out couch on the first floor. He walked into the room swaying from side to side. I left him there and made my way upstairs. Sara was already asleep. I was glad for that. I didn't want to have to talk about Patrick or the past.

Laying my head on the pillow, the entire room

begins to spin and there's a persistent thought in my head that I can't shake. That one night, the night that Patrick reappeared after all those months away, the night that Sara went to him. No matter how hard I push the thought out of my mind, it keeps forcing its way back in.

But I hadn't brought it up again. Not since I placed the ring back onto Sara's finger and she and I put the past behind us. I'd forced the thought away, but now, it was back.

The next morning, I awoke later than usual. Entering the kitchen, my face pale and my eyes red, I go straight for the pills in the cupboard, but Sara's a step ahead. With two pills in one hand and a glass of water in the other, she turns to me.

"Here. Take these."

"Thank you, love."

Popping the pills into my mouth, I notice Patrick out on the deck with a cigarette between his lips. "He's up early."

"No, you're just up late."

"Ah." I pour myself a mug of coffee and take a seat at the kitchen table. "Seems he can still drink me under the table."

"Seems that way," Sara says, standing across from me. "But, you know, considering you have to go to work today..."

"I know," I groan. "I know." Forcing my eyes upwards, I glance out the window once again. "I still can't believe it."

"It is unbelievable, isn't it? After all this time."

The children race into the kitchen, screaming. "Hey, hey." Sara stops them and turns them around. "Go play in the living room. Your father has a headache."

Just then, the porch doors open and Patrick enters with his dimpled smile. "Hey, my favourite little people."

Eric runs towards him shouting, "Help. I'm being chased by a dragon."

Issy sets off after him, her strawberry-brown pigtails flopping about her head. They hang onto Patrick's legs and he picks them up, one in each arm.

"Uncle Patrick," they call out. "You slept here?"

"Aye, I did." He looks at Sara with a smirk. "On that rickety pull-out in your mother's workroom." He then turns to me, saying, "Not that I don't appreciate it. Truth be told, I didn't feel a thing." Patrick laughs, and Eric asks what that means.

"You'll find out one day," he says, lowering the children onto their feet.

"Can you sleep here, always?" Issy asks.

"I don't think your parents would appreciate that so much."

"Why not?" The twins look from me to Sara with pouts on their tiny faces.

"Well..." Patrick puts his hands to his waist and looks thoughtfully at the ceiling. "You see, when two people love each other very much -"

"Okay." Sara cuts him off. "That's enough." She ushers the children towards the kitchen door and again, Eric asks, "What does that mean?"

"Don't worry about it," his mother tells him.

"I'll find out one day?"

The boy's remark, although innocent, sends Patrick into a frenzy of laughter. He throws his head back until tears fill his eyes.

"No..." Sara's gaze falls hard on Patrick's. "It's because Patrick lives with Aunt Rachel and Uncle Frank now, that's why."

Patrick sighs. "I guess I deserve that."

With the children out of the kitchen, and Sara at the counter, Patrick steps up to me. "How's the head?" he asks.

"Not good. Yours?"

"Great. Any plans for today?"

"Work. You?"

He turns towards the yard. "Well, I've been thinking a lot about your yard."

Sara laughs. "That's a strange thing to think about."

Patrick smiles at her. "I'd like to lay some stones out, if you don't mind."

Sipping at my coffee, I grumble, "Seriously?"

"Sure. I'm here. I might as well."

Sara returns with two mugs of coffee. She hands Patrick one of the mugs, then comes to sit across from me.

"You have all that empty green lawn out there," he continues. "It would be nice to have a stone pathway leading from one place to another."

With a smirk, Sara raises her eyebrows to me. I'm thinking the same thing, how long is he planning on staying?

"I'll start at the deck," Patrick explains as he takes a

seat next to Sara. "The path will move along for a few feet. Then it'll split up into two." He draws the design with the tips of his fingers along the kitchen table. "One path will lead towards the shed. The other will move towards the edge of the forest and end at the pond. It would be a nice walk about the grounds."

"When will you have time for this?" I ask.

"I have nothing but time," he says. "I just need to get some supplies, and I'm good to go."

"You don't need to do this," Sara tells him, and Patrick's voice softens.

"I know I don't. But I want to."

The front door to my parent's house swings open. Eric stands in the doorway with his keys in one hand and a stumped look on his face.

"You're home?" he asks.

I leap off the couch feeling a lot like a teenager who's been caught with her pants down. "You have a key?"

He looks down at the set of keys in his palm. "Yeah."

"Why do you have a key? You don't live here."

He averts his eyes to Adrian who's wearing nothing more than the black boxers and an awkward smile. "I knocked," my brother mumbles.

"Honestly." Victoria pushes past her fiancé with a huff. "Mike's here too," she warns.

"Mike?" No.

As announced, Mike appears in the doorway. His eyes meet mine, then shift to the other end of the sofa where Adrian now stands.

"I spilled alcohol on myself," he explains, and I watch as the lines of Mike's forehead begin to form, and the gentle blue eyes harden.

"Relax." Eric slaps Mike on the gut. "It's just underwear."

Mike turns away, brushes off his sneakers, and heads towards the stairs saying, "Let's get this shit over with."

As Mike disappears up the staircase, Eric turns to Adrian and, with that same tone of part amusement, part annoyance, he says, "Dude, put some pants on."

Adrian gives him a thumbs up and heads off towards the laundry room. My brother's glare then turns on me.

"Before you say a word, Sam just broke up with him. He was upset." I say it quickly before he can cut me off.

"So, you entertain him in his underwear?" he snaps.

"Shut up."

"Issy, stop screwing with him."

"What are you talking about."

From upstairs, I can hear furniture scraping across the wooden floor and my brother motions towards the staircase.

"Mike - stop screwing with his mind. He thinks he still has a chance with you, and this weird thing you have going with your gay boyfriend is seriously messing with him."

I flash Eric a hard look and press my lips together so that he can measure the level of my irritation. "Adrian is a friend," I remind him yet again. "And Mike has a new fling so, what does he care?"

"What new fling?"

"The woman from Rosa's, remember?"

"She's not a fling, and so what?"

Victoria leans towards him and whispers, "So, it upset the balance."

"The balance of what?" Eric asks. "The woman's a colleague. They went for lunch together. So what?"

"So, he's going to have to try a hell of a lot harder if he wants to fix this," I tell him. "And I thought you were on my side, anyway."

"I'm not on anyone's side. You're both equally ridiculous."

I scoff and turn away.

"And you're a damn hypocrite too," he bellows after me.

"Excuse me?" I turn around abruptly to find my brother's finger pointed at my face.

"Look, let me put this into perspective for you since you live in a fishbowl." I roll my eyes at him. "At dinner the other day, Mike entered the house just as you went off to the kitchen. He greeted everyone, then he went off to talk to you." He leans towards me. "Adrian's eyes were on him the whole time."

"And?"

"And the guy nearly leapt off his chair after him."

I knit my eyebrows with growing agitation. "What are you implying?"

"Adrian's your emotional buffer."

"Oh, please." I flop down onto the couch.

"He's the guy you go to when you're feeling sad and lonely."

"Whatever."

"When you need a shoulder to lean on." Eric slides down next to me, forcing me to push over. "When you need a hug."

"I get it."

"You've substituted Mike for Adrian."

"No, I haven't."

"Yes, you have."

"You're ridiculous."

Victoria comes to sit next to me. "Honey." She places a hand over mine. "I'm sorry, but he's right."

Just then, Mike comes stomping down the stairs.

"Great." I jump to my feet and hurry through the kitchen door before he can catch the dismay on my face.

Out on the deck, I stare out to the forest ahead. What the hell are they going on about? I'm not substituting Mike with anyone, because no one can replace what we had or what we've been through together, and no one ever will.

"Issy." The patio doors open and Mike steps out with a glower on his face. "Are you going to tell me what the hell is going on between the two of you?"

I look up to the sky before turning my attention to him. "Mike, you need to stop this."

He comes to stand over me. "What am I supposed to think when I see the man standing there in his underwear?"

"Honestly, Mike, think what you want. You will anyway."

He lets out a loud puff. I realize now would be a good time to tell him that my personal life is none of his business. What I do or don't do with Adrian doesn't concern him in the least. But as he stands there watching me with that accusatory look on his face, I know that it's utterly futile.

"Listen..." Mike's tone softens. "I don't want to fight." He takes hold of my hands. "I meant what I said. You're the girl I want to be with. There's no one else." He leans in close, his blue eyes gazing into mine. "It's you... it's only you."

Looking up at him, I'm reminded of the gentleness of those blue eyes. That's what caught my attention. The first time I met Mike, we were in high school. I was sitting at Rosa's Café when a tall, broad-shouldered boy approached me. Standing over me, he asked, "Are you Eric's sister?"

I nodded shyly.

He shook my hand and introduced himself. Then, with a soft smile, he said, "You're a lot cuter than your twin."

It made me laugh.

The patio doors open again. This time, Eric appears with a couple of beers in his hands.

"Hey, man." He passes Mike a bottle, then turns to me saying, "I didn't think you'd want one."

"I don't – and neither should you."

Eric flashes me one of his sly smirks, takes a seat on a deck chair, and starts guzzling back the beer.

"So, you're heading back to Ottawa straight from here?" Mike asks.

"Yup."

"Wait. You're leaving today?"

"Day four," Eric reminds me. "Thank fuck."

"Unnecessary," Victoria remarks as she joins us, followed by Adrian who is now back into his clothes.

"But..." I glance from Victoria to Eric. "You can't leave."

"Why not?" Victoria asks, settling herself onto my brother's lap.

"Because, I need to talk to you."

Eric flashes me a curious look. "About what?"

I fall silent. I don't even know where to start.

"Well, it can wait," he decides. "Call me on the road. I'll be on it for the next four hours." He looks up at the cloudless sky with a sigh. "Plenty of time to chat."

Eric takes another drink and, suddenly, his brow deepens. "By the way, where did mom and dad F-off to?"

I shrug. "Mom said they were going back home. To a funeral."

"Hm." My brother presses his lips together. It's

clear that he has a suspicion which, as I well know, will always lead to the need for an answer.

"Why do you ask?"

"I don't know..." He takes another sip. "Mom called me on the way to the airport but refused to give me details. It was weird."

"Speaking of which," Victoria adds. "We'd better be on our way if we want to avoid rush hour traffic."

"Yes." Eric finishes the beer and gets to his feet "Oh, and Issy, try not to kill the cat, will you."

What a thing to say. "Why would I kill the cat?"

"There was no food in his bowl. Or water. I filled them for you. You're welcome."

Crap, I completely forgot.

As everyone scuttles back into the house, Mike takes my hand and we linger back a moment.

"When are you getting this off?" he asks, placing a hand under my bandaged arm.

I look down at the wrapping on my arm. "About a week or so." Except that I'm not ready to expose the stitches yet.

He slides his hand along my arm. "Can I call you sometime?"

My gaze drifts across his chest, then up to his smiling eyes. I nod. I miss him.

After they leave, Adrian and I settle back onto the sofa with the photographs. "So..." He nudges me with an elbow. "You and Mike, huh?"

I grimace. "I don't know." I'm not going to speculate nor presume that everything will be okay.

We still have things to discuss.

"Well, good thing he doesn't know that I slept in your bed last night?" He laughs as he flips through the photos, and I roll my eyes at him.

"By the way..." Adrian holds up the picture of Patrick sitting on the unknown couch in the mystery apartment. "You should reach out to this aunt of yours. See what she knows. I mean, she's the only other person in these photos. She must know the story behind the fight, and what happened to the guy, right?"

"Patrick, you mean."

"Yeah. The one that vanished."

The comment sparks an idea. I stare back at him, eyes wide, and Adrian gives me that look, the one where he imitates my expression knowing he's not going to be able to stop what comes next.

Turning around, I race up the stairs and head for my bedroom.

"Issy." Adrian chases after me. "What are you doing?"

Seated at my desk, I get onto my laptop and start typing.

He leans over me, gawking at the screen. "Are you out of your mind? You have no business going over there."

I gape up at him in awe, and he retracts the comment.

"Okay, I get it. You want to see him. You need closure. But, Issy..." He pulls my hands away from the keyboard. "Booking a flight to Europe on a whim is not the answer. What if you don't like what you find when you get there?"

I know what he means, but I have to try.

When I refuse to give up on the idea, Adrian tosses his credit card onto my desk and says, "Fine. Book me in too then."

"You don't have to do this."

He swivels my chair around, leans over me, and says, "You think I'm going to let you go through this alone?"

CHAPTER 22   October 1996

Nearing six o'clock, I pull into the driveway to find Sara and Patrick arguing at the rear of her vehicle. Rachel stands aside, looking on in amusement.

"I told you to leave them be." Patrick forcibly yanks the bags from Sara's grasp. "I said I'd come back for them."

"I'm not helpless, you know?"

"Aye, I know you're not helpless."

"Then stop treating me like I am."

Patrick sighs and walks on ahead with several grocery bags in each hand.

"Sara," I call to her before she can go after him. "What's going on?"

"He thinks I'm helpless," she shouts in Patrick's direction. "He thinks I can't do anything myself."

"I know you can," Patrick calls back from the porch steps. "But I preferred you didn't."

She throws her arms in the air and gawks at me. "You see?"

"I'd let him do it." Rachel's standing close by with her hands pressed to her hips and her eyes on Patrick's backside as he struts away. "I mean, just look at him go."

"Rachel." Sara scolds her. "Seriously?"

"What? I have eyes," she shoots back. "And my eyes like to look at his rear."

Patrick, overhearing them, turns around. With a sultry gaze and a dimpled smile, he bows and utters a humbled, "It's my pleasure, m' lady."

I smirk at him.

Sara questioned her aunt the evening before, while Patrick ran around the yard with the twins, asking how she could keep Patrick's whereabouts from her.

"It was for your own good," her aunt assured her. "He couldn't come back, and you needed to get over him. So, it was for the best."

I agreed.

After dinner, while Sara and Rachel head into the yard with the twins. Patrick and I remain on the deck discussing the progress of the new stone path.

"I just need to set the gravel," Patrick says. "Then I'll be ready to lay down the stones."

"You just let me know if you need more supplies,"

I tell him.

He reaches into his back pocket and lights a cigarette. "Will do."

Yesterday, when he pulled out the cigarette pack, I asked him when he started smoking. Patrick told me, "Since I was forced to kill a man with m' bare hands."

That'll do it, I'd thought.

Leaning against the railing, I stare down at the burning cigarette between my fingers and ask, "How did you do it?"

Patrick turns to me with a blank expression. He knows damn well what I'm talking about.

"Well..." Resting his elbows on the railing, he says, "I got him to follow me to the border of Quebec." He takes a long drag of the cigarette and lowers his head. "I stopped at some dive motel at the side of the highway. It was mostly truckers and such. Figured it was a good place to end it."

"End it?"

"I knew I had to get rid of him. One way or another, he had to go." He pauses a moment, as though calculating the events in his mind. "Sometime after midnight, I caught the bastard creeping along the hallway looking into people's rooms. So, I opened the door to let him see me. Then, I went back inside and waited for him."

He shrugs and takes another puff. "Figured it couldn't be too hard, the man didn't look well."

I narrow my gaze in question and he tells me that one side of Devons face was disfigured.

"And he was limpin' something awful," Patrick

recalls.

He takes a deep breath and shakes his head, adding, "You guys made it look so damn easy." I can see the regret on his face. "I'm not proud of it, you know."

"We seldom are," I tell him but, sometimes, there's no other way around it.

Then, rather unexpectedly, he says, "Did you ever feel like you were nearing your end?"

"What kind of shit is that?"

"I don't know. Just a feeling." He butts out the cigarette and changes the subject. "Anyway, Rachel found out about it and decided to put me up in her apartment. That's where I've been."

"How did that come about?"

"I called the shop one day. I was trying to get a hold of Sara, to tell her that I was leaving. I didn't know where, but I knew I couldn't stick around here. But Rachel refused to let me talk to her." He grins. "She insisted on knowing what was going on. I tried to give her the same story you told her about the new job out west, but she wouldn't have it." He chuckles to himself, but the amusement soon fades. "Said she already knew most of it."

"She has a way of getting these things out of you."

"No kidding. It was like I was at confession. I told her everything."

"Everything?"

He nods.

"And she still let you see her?"

"Hell, no. I tried again and again. Eventually, I got

through to Sara."

I can't help but wonder if that's the day she went to him.

"I called you too," he says.

"Yeah? When?"

"That same day. I called the apartment. I tried your office. You didn't answer."

"The last time I heard from you was July, a couple of months after you took off," I tell him. "You left me a message talking about how you'd made it to Quebec. That Devons was gone."

Patrick nods. "Aye, I called you right after I got rid of him..." He lowers his head. "But that's not what I'm talking about. I'm talking months later, soon after the new year. I was holed up in some dive motel for weeks, afraid to come out, afraid they'd find me."

"I don't remember getting a call, or a message."

"I was afraid to leave a message in case they'd catch on to you."

Jaw clenched, I toss my cigarette and pull off from the railing. "I don't hear from you for five years and, now, you show up and tell me that you were afraid to leave me a message?"

"I know. It's crazy."

"It's a little more than crazy, Patrick. It's bullshit." The anger resonates on multiple levels. First, there's Sara and all the memories that follow her and Patrick. Then, there's friendship and brotherhood and betrayal. "Five years, mate." I stare across at him, bewildered by the bullshit he's feeding me. "I thought you were dead."

"I'm sorry. I couldn't risk it. I didn't know how close they were to finding me out. I couldn't lead them back to you. Or Sara. That's why I had her come to me."

I turn my gaze towards the thickness of the forest where the autumn leaves have begun to come in. Why the hell did he have to bring this shit up?

"After Rachel offered me the apartment, I went into the city, close to the airport..." He pauses, and I take a deep breath. "Anyway, I didn't do it just for my sake." I wish he'd shut up. "I did it for you and Sara too."

"Right." He sure as hell didn't sleep with my fiancée for my sake.

He looks out into the yard. "And the children."

The comment makes my blood curdle. I can't get those words out of my mind.

Five days later, the stone path is complete. One pathway reaches out to the shed, then continues onto the end of the yard towards the edge of the forest where it coils like a snake. The second path slithers along the grass until it reaches the pond and it too coils around the small body of water where two benches have been placed. The children race back and forth, jumping over the stones with their swords and shields.

"It looks great," I tell him.

"It's beautiful, Patrick," Rachel says. "Really beautiful."

Sara, seated on one of the deck chairs, turns to Patrick at her side. "Thank you for this."

He reaches over and touches his glass to hers. "It was nothing. Only took a few scraped knuckles and some blood loss. Nothing a little alcohol can't fix."

Rachel laughs.

"And the children love those shields you made for them," Sara says, pouring herself another drink of Sangria, made by Patrick himself.

"Well, Eric's sword is looking a little floppy," Patrick notes from his chair. "I'll have to make him a new one."

"Yes, you have to." Sara rises and calls out to Eric. In that moment, she loses her footing and Patrick catches her.

"Woah." He eases her back onto her chair. Then, sliding the glass from her hand, he says, "That's enough for you, m' lady."

"Excuse me, Mr. O'Reilly," she teases, reaching out for her glass. "I'll drink if I want to drink."

"Really?" He chuckles as he pulls the glass further from her reach. "You can barely stand."

"You know, you never used to be so bossy," she says.

"And you never used to be such a light-weight."

I watch them from across the deck, observing in silence.

"Well, this isn't your home." Sara continues to joke with him. "And you, Mr. O'Reilly, are not my husband."

Patrick leans over her and, with his face close to hers, I hear him say, "No, I'm not, am I?"

Sara and Patrick had warmed up to one another

over the past couple of days. No longer arguing, they spoke quietly together. It irked me at times but, in these moments, I reminded myself that Sara is my wife, and soon Patrick will be gone. Yet, I continue to observe.

"Mommy!" Issy's cries ring out. The girl comes racing onto the deck in her green coat and her little hands cupped together with a small winged creature. "Eric killed a butterfly."

"I didn't mean it," he shouts, storming after her. "It was an accident."

Issy can't contain her sorrow and Patrick leaps to the little girl's aid. Gently, he takes the butterfly from her tiny hands and says, "You know what? I think we should have a proper burial for this little guy because you know what happens when we bury him?" He leans close to her ear as though he's about to tell her a secret. The children's eyes grow wide with anticipation. "He's reborn into a new butterfly."

Issy's sweet brown eyes light up. "Really?"

"Come along." Patrick takes hold of her hand into his. "I'll show you what I mean. You too, Eric."

The three march to the end of the yard by the forest where they bury the butterfly.

We arrive in Lisbon on a cloudy day filled with salty ocean mist. From the airport, we travel by train and catch a glimpse of Mediterranean life as we breeze along the oceanside. Forty minutes later, we arrive at our destination.

The nine-story building with the iron balconies and the narrow front door looks to be about one hundred years old. Stepping inside, the cracks on the walls and the uneven wooden stairs provide further proof of the ageing structure.

Ascending the narrow steps, Adrian slips and I turn around to find him hanging on to the railing and the wall like a spider monkey with all four limbs rigid and spread outward.

"I'm okay," he says. "Carry on."

With a steady hand on the railing, I continue to climb.

After what feels like an infinite amount of time, we arrive on the sixth floor. I knock on the door and then, we wait. Two minutes later, I hear the click of the lock and my aunt appears in the doorway looking utterly stumped.

"Isabella?"

"Aunt Rachel. Hi."

She looks aged and her skin seems pale against the black sleeveless dress.

"What are you doing here?" she asks, and my smile recedes. It's been close to ten years since I've seen my aunt. I'd hoped for a better reception.

"I called," I tell her.

"When?"

"Six days ago. I spoke to Frank." Adrian and I are still standing in the hallway.

My aunt's face stiffens and, with her hands at her hips, she starts to curse under her breath.

"I take it he didn't tell you?"

"No."

My face falls, and I lower my small suitcase onto the floor. "I'm sorry..." I don't know what else to say and now I'm wondering if Adrian was right. Maybe this was a mistake.

"Oh, goodness." My aunt throws a couple of bare flappy arms into the air and pulls me into her large breasts. "Come here. No need to be sorry. I'm happy you're here." She then turns to Adrian saying, "Come in, come in."

Ushering us through the long and narrow living room, I take note of the brown sofa and the picture frame of the cobblestones and shops on the wall. This is the same living room from the photograph... we were here.

As we enter the kitchen, Rachel asks what brings us all the way here and I notice that the concerned expression hasn't left her face. When I show her the photo of us with Patrick seated in her living room, my aunt's frown deepens.

She takes it into her hands and her eyes begin to glisten. "Does your mother know that you're here?"

I shake my head. "She doesn't know I know."

There's a hint of reluctance as she asks, "Know what?"

"About Patrick - that he's my father."

"Oh, Issy." She takes hold of my hand. "I wish you'd spoken to your mother before coming."

There's a pang in my heart and the terrible feeling that's been with me since I left home grows.

"I'm so sorry," she continues. "But you're two weeks too late."

I feel Adrian's eyes on me.

"Patrick's gone," my aunt utters the words in a whisper. "Your parents just left last night."

"My parents?"

"Yes, they were here for the funeral."

I feel as though I've been hit in the gut by a fast-moving baseball.

"Come." She takes me by the shoulders and sits me at the table. "You have a seat here beside her," she tells Adrian, pulling a chair out for him. "I'll make us some coffee."

As the water boils, my aunt busies herself setting the table with flowery dessert plates and matching mugs. A short white porcelain jar of milk and a container of sugar are placed in front of us. She then sets a loaf of bread on the table along with an assortment of cheeses.

While my aunt continues to fuss about, I sit in silence staring blankly at the table. I can't believe he's gone... I had so many questions.

My aunt settles across from us with a silver kettle and a jar of instant coffee. As she looks over at me, I can't hold back the tears that rise into my eyes and spill onto my cheeks.

She sets the pot down. "Issy..."

"They should have said something. They should have told us." The ache in my throat forces me into silence.

"I know that this is hard," my aunt tells me. "But you have to understand the situation."

"Oh, I do understand," I slap away the tears. "That's the problem. I know that my mother dated Patrick when she was young. And I know that after Patrick left, my parents got together. I also know that Patrick returned sometime in the new year, or else we can't possibly belong to him." My voice rises in agitation. "And I also know that my parents were already engaged when my mother went off and screwed him. Isn't that about right?"

My aunt leans back in her chair and folds her arms in front of her chest. "Yes, if you want to be vulgar about it, yes. But your mother loved Patrick."

I stare back at her, insulted by the statement.

"Issy." My aunt looks across the table at me with a sympathetic gaze. "Patrick left so suddenly. There was so much left unsaid. When he returned, it was only for one night and it was only to see her. He wanted to explain to her why he had to go away. You can imagine the emotions."

"But she was already engaged."

"Yes, she was."

I scoff at the thought of it. "No wonder my father beat the crap out of him."

"Isabella -" Her first instinct is to reprimand me, but she stops herself. "You remember that?"

I nod. "I saw it." There was blood everywhere. It was horrible. My brother and I stood with our small hands pressed to the cold glass of the French doors. We saw the whole thing. I remember the red blotches scattered on the snowy deck, like red paint splatter.

My aunt wraps her hands around her mug. "I can assure you that Patrick didn't deserve that."

I press my lips together and glare at her, certain that she's wrong. "Why did they fight then?"

She shrugs her shoulders. "Blinding love and fairytale delusions." She looks away then and the sadness returns to her eyes. "And Patrick should have never challenged your father like that."

"That piece of shit!"

Storming across the kitchen, I find him on the deck with a cigarette to his lips.

"David. Please." Sara's chasing after me, but there's no use. I couldn't contain the rage if I wanted to.

Throwing the patio doors open, I bolt across the deck towards Patrick. "What the hell did you say to my kids?"

He tosses his cigarette onto the snow and holds his palm out to me. "David, wait."

I slap his hand away. "They came to me crying. They think they're going away to live with you and their mother. What the hell are you thinking?"

"They're not yours," he swallows hard. "They

belong with me."

"You god-damned bastard." As if the thought hasn't pressed upon me every damn day since they were born. "I've raised those kids since birth. I fed them, clothed them, cared for them, so don't you tell me they're not mine."

Patrick's gaze shifts to Sara. "Go get them ready. Go now."

"Are you out of your fucking mind?"

I feel Sara's hand on my arm and, as I turn to look at her, her tearful eyes meet mine. "David." She shakes her head at me. "Let's go inside and talk."

I stare back at her, uncertain what to think. She wouldn't run off with him. Not now. Not after five years. Then again, I'd never imagined that she would have slept with him after she'd agreed to marry me.

"I should have never left her here -" he stammers. "I should have never left her here with you." He's always been too damn emotional. It was his downfall. "I should have taken her with me."

"She's not a dog, you damn oaf. And if she wanted to be with you, she would have gone with you."

"I love her."

I clench my fists.

"I've always loved her."

I tear away from Sara's grasp and shove Patrick hard with both palms across his chest.

Patrick stumbles and catches himself. "Right. I almost forgot." He comes to stand in front of me with more confidence than before. "Once you get going, there's no stopping you, is there?"

"Shut your mouth."

"That's the old David I remember, raging beyond reason. Like trying to reason with a python who's got you half-way down its throat, that's what the guys used to say. Did you ever tell her about those days?"

"I'm warning you."

"How many guys did you send to the hospital? How many others were sent into retirement at your hands? Did you ever tell her about the horrible person you once were?"

"You piece of shit!"

The force of the hit throws Patrick onto the ground. He tries to get up, but I move over him. As my fists come down on his face, blinding rage takes over every sense. Over and over, I pound on him until his body goes limp.

"Stop." Sara throws herself over me. "David. Stop." She clings to my arm, shouting, "You're going to kill him."

Looking down at Patrick's bludgeoned face, I regain control of myself.

"What have you done?" Sara rushes to his side and I move away. "What is wrong with you?"

I stare back at her, my body tense and my breaths coming fast while I try to calm the rage inside. No matter what comes out of my mouth, I know I'll regret it so, I turn around and walk back into the house. Seated on the black leather sofa in my office, I wait for whatever comes next.

By the time the ambulance arrives, Rachel and Frank are at the house. Still in my office, I sit with my elbows to my knees and my head lowered.

The office door opens. "David," Rachel calls to me from the doorway. "I'm taking Sara to the hospital," she says.

I don't respond.

"Frank will take the kids to our place for a little while... give you some time to yourself."

I turn my face away from her and she murmurs a hurried good-bye and shuts the door again.

Ever since Patrick walked in through the front door, my mind has been on edge battling through a twisted dystopia of emotions: agitation, remorse, resentment. I couldn't pinpoint the exact word, but I knew that it was somewhere in there. To think that he'd been plotting to run off with my wife and kids, I wanted to kill him. If she hadn't stopped me, I might have.

Nearing three o'clock in the afternoon, Sara returns. I'm still in my office.

"Patrick's regained consciousness," she says.

I remain as I am, seated over the couch nursing my wounds with an ice pack to my knuckles and a glass of cognac on the coffee table.

"You're lucky he's not pressing charges," she says, taking another step into the room. "David. How can you do that to him?" Her tone grows severe and I raise my eyes to meet hers. "How can you be so cruel?"

"You're asking me how I can be so cruel?"

Sara stares back at me, tears filling her eyes. "He'll never be the same again."

"I don't care."

"How can you say that? Are you seriously incapable of showing any remorse? Or compassion? He's your friend. He's been like a brother to you."

For five years, I've buried all notions of the truth, the aching possibility that my children weren't mine. Every time that someone remarked on the strawberry tint in Issy's hair and Eric's blue-green eyes with that hint of grey, I swatted away their insinuations. "They don't look so much like you," people would say. My first reaction was to send them all to hell. Instead, I'd bite my tongue and jokingly tell them that it was the mailman. They'd get a good laugh out of that and shut up about it.

Fact of the matter is, I've always known it. I knew that they were his and not mine. Sara and I never said it out loud, as though silencing the truth might erase it from existence. Regardless, I'd raised them and loved them as though they were my own.

"David." Sara's standing in front of me. "Are you listening?"

"Five years, Sara." I'm on my feet, heat rising into my face and rage filling my veins. "He shows up after five years, tries to take everything from me, and I'm supposed to just sit here and take it?"

"You almost killed him."

"He deserved it."

Her lip quivers. "Patrick's lying in a hospital bed right now, barely able to hold a conversation. He's ruined because of you and, still, you can't show an ounce of remorse. Is this who you are?"

In an explosive fit of rage, I squeeze the ice pack in my fist and whip it across the room. The pack hits the wall and ruptures into a blast of ice chips. "Isn't that what he did to me? Didn't he ruin me just the same?"

"No, David," she utters with tears racing down her cheeks. "He didn't ruin you. You've done it to yourself."

The words hit me hard, tearing deep into me.

Later that evening, Rachel calls me. She tells me that Sara and the twins are at her place.

"I've told her to keep this between us," she says. "No one else needs to know what happened today."

She then tells me that the truth always comes out. One way or another. "You just need to face it, overcome it, and decide if you're okay with the new version of the truth that you've been dealt. I've said the same to Sara. Now, it's up to the two of you to figure it out."

The past echoes in my mind.

Adrian and I walk along the pier where the ocean meets the sand and extends across the train tracks. While he stops to buy a cold drink from a vendor, I pace ahead towards a nearby bench. A group of young men dance along the boardwalk to the sounds of Brazilian samba. Swirling around passers-by, one man takes an older woman by the hand. She laughs as he spins her.

On his way back to me, a can of soda in his hand, Adrian becomes caught in the whirlwind of dancers. Now, he too is swept away, spinning and laughing and swaying. I smile to see him, but my thoughts are elsewhere.

§

"Your mother never counted on falling in love with David," my aunt told me while we sat at the table, once more decorated with porcelain dinnerware filled with fresh bread, cheese, and mugs of coffee. "But she did," she added, "and your parents built a beautiful life together."

My aunt carried on, her hands clasped over the table, and a weary look on her face. "And David was right, you know. You and your brother are as much his as you are Patrick's. David raised you from birth. He cared for you and loved you." She raises a hand to her face as though wiping away the exhaustion. "Patrick had no right to think that he could just show up and take it all away."

I felt for my father then, and I almost justified the fight until my aunt told me about the concussions.

"Patrick suffered through several," she said. "They occurred during his boxing career, mostly." As she continued the story about the multiple concussions, the doctor visits, the fear that the next one might very well kill him, I begin to paint a dark picture.

"Don't get me wrong," she told me, her hands reaching for mine as though to provide me greater comfort of the horrid tale. "Your father loved Patrick like a brother, right down to his final days."

"But he knew how fragile Patrick was," I had said.

She lowered her eyes from mine then and uttered a sorrowful, "Yes."

"And he fought him anyway."

A nod followed.

"Why?" I asked, still unable to believe that my

father was capable of such cruelty. "Why did he do it?"

My aunt shrugged, suggesting that it was all on account of uncontainable rage.

"You make my father sound like a monster." I refused to accept it.

My aunt, frowning, tells me, "No, of course, he's not a monster. But Patrick knew what your father was like."

"What does that mean?"

My aunt began to smooth out the embroidered tablecloth with the tips of her fingers. "That fight destroyed Patrick," she went on to tell me through dampened eyes. "He was never the same after that."

But it was the trembling, she said, the inability to hold a conversation, or take a few steps without having to hold onto a piece of furniture, those things got to him most. "And that is why they kept Patrick a secret. Because your father couldn't come to terms with what he'd done to his friend. They kept it from you to protect you from knowing the truth."

For a long while afterwards, I'd stood in the living room looking out through the square window with the wooden panels. Ahead, the ocean waves crashed against the stone wall barrier. It didn't take me long to realize that this is the place where it all began.

Soon after our fourth birthday, my brother and I travelled here with our mother. We'd spent an entire month in this little town on the outskirts of Lisbon while Patrick tried to recover. Then, we left and we never saw Patrick again.

This is where the problems began: the anxiousness, the inability to trust and to love without reservation, the fear of losing another person that I care about. It began here in this apartment overlooking the Atlantic all those years ago.

§

Adrian's laughter draws my attention back into the present and I gaze across the pier to where he stands chatting with a young dark man.

"Okay," I hear Adrian say, "I'm going this way now." As he steps away, the man reaches out and slaps Adrian hard across the rear. Adrian glances over his shoulder with a smile.

Approaching me, the smile still on his face, he takes my hand and we head down the pier to await the train.

"What was that all about?" I ask.

"I think he wanted to take me home."

"Interesting."

A mischievous grin comes over him. "He is."

The train soon pulls up with a final puff and an abrupt halt. Standing in front of the open door, Adrian asks, "Are you sure you want to do this?"

"Yes. That's why we're here, right?"

§

Patrick lived out his final years in a small cottage up in the mountains. "His family still lives out in that cottage," my aunt had said.

With curiosity pecking at my mind, I had turned to Adrian and asked, "Will you go with me?"

"Of course," he responded without hesitation. "Isn't that's why we came all the way out here - on a whim?"

I smirked at him, and my aunt started across the living room saying, "I'll make a phone call."

Approaching the townhouse, I can hear the twins running inside. They're shouting after one another and laughing together. For a moment, I stop and smile. Then, the door opens, and I'm met by Frank's scruffy black beard and matching dark eyes.

"Hi, Frank."

"You're not going to cause any trouble, I hope." His lips are pressed behind that mess of a beard.

"No, Frank."

"Daddy." The twins run up to me and I wrap them into my arms. I miss their little voices.

"He's in the kitchen," Frank tells me as he takes the children by the hand saying, "Let's go outside and play while daddy and Uncle Patrick have a chat." He halts half-way out the door. "I'll be right outside."

It was a warning. "Got it, Frank."

Making my way towards the kitchen, I find Patrick standing by the counter in his Tartan pyjama pants and a white short-sleeve shirt.

He looks frail. Slightly hunched over and holding onto the edge of the counter, he turns to looks at me. "What the hell are you doing here?"

"I'm just here to talk."

"You don't have a phone?"

I grin to myself while Patrick moves towards the kitchen table with an empty glass and a bottle of his favourite Irish whiskey.

Glancing down at his bare feet and the unsteady gait, I ask him how he's doing. The question causes instant agitation.

"How the hell do you think I'm doing?" Patrick snaps and, when I don't respond, he says, "Right, nothing at all to do with Sara."

Sara had asked me to come and talk to him. Make amends, is what she said. So, here I was, watching Patrick's hands tremble while he struggles to twist the cap off the bottle.

"Do you need help with that?"

"No, I don't need your damn help." Finally, he manages to remove the cap from the bottle, and it clangs against the glass.

"So..." He sets the bottle down and takes back the shot of liquor. "Come to finish the job, have you?"

I sigh; he pours himself another drink.

"Aye, I get it. Killer's remorse."

With a chuckle, I take a seat across from him. Patrick had become rather amusing. "Like I said, I'm just here to talk, that's all."

A loud laugh erupts from Patrick's throat. "I'm right? You do feel guilty." Patrick takes back the shot and proceeds to pour himself a third.

"Look, I took it too far. You know I didn't mean it."

The shift in Patrick's eyes is instant, and he slams the bottle onto the table. "You didn't mean to ruin my life? Is that it? Well, good for you. Except that it's too late for remorse ol' friend 'cause you screwed me good. I guess it's fair though, isn't it? I screw you. You screw me. Guess we're even, aren't we?"

He lifts the bottle and it slips from his hand and the alcohol spills onto the table. In a fit of rage, Patrick picks up the glass and whips it across the room. It shatters against the far wall. "Do you see what you've done," he erupts, slamming his fist over the table. "You fucked me is what you've done."

I stare at him. The once gentle husky Irishman had turned into a brooding tempered drunk, but the outburst didn't faze me. Rather, it was the insinuation that I too hadn't suffered that infuriated me.

"What the hell did you think was going to happen?" I snap back. "What were you thinking coming here, trying to take everything from me?"

"Everything you have is a lie," he says. "Your house, your fancy truck, your job. All of it, courtesy of dirty money and lies. Even your kids aren't yours."

I rise to my feet and lean towards him, my knuckles

pressed to the table. "Listen to me, you damn bastard. Yes, I came here because she asked me to. I didn't have to. And I'm not sure you deserve it, so don't make me regret it."

Patrick waves his hand at me. "Whatever, I don't give a shit. Leave - don't leave. I've already got one foot in the grave. Figure I'll go all out from here on in."

With great restraint, I ease myself back onto the chair.

"You know..." Patrick takes his seat, raises the bottle to his lips, then slams it down again. "The difference between you and me, chum, is that I'm not afraid to tell her about my past. You can't even be honest about who you are."

"That's bullshit and you know it. When the hell did you ever tell her the truth?"

Patrick grimaces. "That night, at the hotel, I told her everything. I told her about the fights. How you brought me in. I only didn't tell her about your past because I thought you'd already done it, stupid bloke."

"Yeah? Did you tell her about Devons? What we did? What you did? You couldn't, could you? Because you knew she'd never forgive you for it."

"Aye, I started to," he says with a grunt as he tries to steady himself onto his feet. "But I stopped myself."

"I know."

Patrick glances across at me, somewhat surprised.

"She told me about it. She said you started to talk about what happened that night at Barton's estate. She wanted to know more, but I told her I didn't know anything about it." A grin comes over me. "You think we'd be married for five years and she wouldn't tell me?"

Patrick's gaze lowers from mine and his face falls. Holding onto the back of the chair, he turns towards the kitchen and I rise before he can take a step. With a hand to his shoulder, I tell him to sit.

In the kitchen, I grab a couple of glasses from a cupboard. "It's probably best that you didn't," I tell him as I set the glasses onto the table and pour a shot into each one. "It would have only hurt her." Then, raising my glass to him, I tell him, "Drink up, mate. This will be your last for a while."

Patrick frowns at me. "What the hell are you talking about?"

"I need you sober."

"Why?"

"Because you're going into therapy."

He snickers. "Therapy? What therapy?"

A sigh escapes me. He was right. The guilt ate away at me. "I want to help you."

"You want to help me?"

"Yes."

A twisted frown appears over Patrick's face. "You do this to me and then you want to help me?"

"I didn't do this to you," I tell him. "It was already there."

"Aye, but you threw the last hit, didn't you? Even though you knew what it would do to me. But David Bauer doesn't have regrets, right? He acts and reacts however his emotions guide him."

I glare across the table at him. I'd been battling

between blame and an overactive ego. Truth of it was, the guilt had gotten to me. "I'm sorry. Alright?"

Patrick's gaze widens as though filled with a sudden revelation. "This is priceless. Six years I've known you, mate, and you've never admitted to anything, let alone apologized for it."

I remain silent and Patrick bursts into laughter. He hits the table with the palm of his hand. "You're a twisted son of a bitch, you know that?"

It's after midnight when Sara enters my office. I'd been lying over the sofa for hours with the lights turned off while she rummaged around upstairs. Now, as she enters the room, I lift my arm from my face and glance across at her.

"I'm sorry I woke you," she says.

"I wasn't sleeping." Rising, I go to the desk and turn on the lamp. Then, turning to look at her, I notice the dark shadows under her eyes. "Are you alright?"

Sara lowers her gaze from mine. "I don't want you to get upset..."

Over her shoulder, out in the hallway, I see the large black suitcase. "Where are you going?"

"David..." Her eyes begin to gloss over.

"You're leaving?"

"Just for a little while."

The heavy feeling from earlier fills my chest once again. "Where?"

"Europe." She hands me a small note. "Rachel and Frank will need help."

I cross my arms over my chest. "You mean Patrick

needs help." She doesn't answer. "How long?"

"I'm not sure yet."

"Hm." I unfold the piece of paper. Scribbled in Sara's handwriting is the phone number and address to Rachel and Frank's apartment in Portugal.

"And the twins?" I ask.

Sara chokes on her words, "They're coming with me."

"I see." I lift the small piece of paper between two fingers. "Thanks for this."

She nods and, as she turns to leave, I ask, "Are you coming back?"

I watch as tears spill onto her cheeks. "I don't know."

That night, I feel a deep burden weighing over me. Laying alone in our bed, I think how ironic it is that I should lie here in the place where we've slept and laughed and made love.

"What is wrong with you?" Sara's words continue to echo in my ears. What is wrong with me? I've asked myself that same question over and over since the fight. I can't come up with an answer. I know I took it too far but damn him. What the hell was Patrick thinking?

Lying awake late into the night, I think through the losses in my life. I think of my mother and the pain I felt to have lost her, and the sadness of being separated from my brothers. Then, I think of my father. The man had loathed himself so much that he couldn't possibly love anyone else.

When I left home, I told myself that I would never be like him. I promised myself that if I ever had a family,

I would raise my children in the very opposite way of my father, and I would ensure that my wife felt loved. But now, here I was in this dark and empty house feeling regretful and alone and, I can't help but wonder if I'm the cause of all my losses.

Exasperated, I place my forearm across my eyes and weep.

Chapter 27   September 2016

It felt as though we had been driving in circles for hours. The bus veers from left to right, up and down, but always climbing. At one point, we pull into a tunnel and everything becomes so dark that I can't make out the faces of the people around me. Then, as we barrel back out of that hole in the earth, everything becomes bright again and I close my eyes and readjust to the light.

All the while the bus keeps climbing, hugging the mountainside so close that I can reach out and touch the earth. Outside of the adjacent windows, there is nothing but blue sky as the cliff descends just feet from the narrow dirt road.

Moments later, we come to an abrupt halt and everyone is led off the bus. I'm filled with relief for this pause in the journey. After four hours of ascension, the countless scents from the hundreds of plants and flowers have become so overwhelming that I feel like I'm going to be sick.

Everyone piles into a small white stone building with a single rusted metal door and a hole in the wall for a window. It looks like something out of a horror movie.

Adrian turns to me with a shrug. "When in Rome?"

I sigh. "Why do I feel like we're never going to come back out?"

Laughing, he pulls me along.

Inside the single room, the fluorescent lighting makes me feel as though I've been transported back in time. The shop is plain with white walls, a single glass refrigerator, and a shelf unit that holds a mash-up of items for grabs from chocolate bars to condoms to pain medication I've never heard of.

Behind a shabby wooden desk stands a tall, lean man with wiry hair and dark stubble on a deeply creased face. Were it not for his bright eyes, and the strength of his posture, I would think he was pushing seventy.

Adrian and I pick up a couple of bottles of water, bags of chips, and chocolate bars. At the cash register, the attendant offers us cigarettes and booze.

"No, thank you. Just this," I tell him while my stomach grumbles.

In the four hours that we've spent travelling up this god-forsaken mountain, we hadn't hit a single restaurant. People had packed lunches of large doughy buns with ham and cheese and mustard. They ate with smiles on their faces, licking their lips and fingers, while Adrian and I salivated.

My aunt had offered us sandwiches too, but we refused them saying we'd pick something up on the way.

"Make sure you do," she said, "Or you'll starve before you get there." Figuring she was being melodramatic, I ignored her warning and now found myself gobbling down my chocolate bar like a child who had never tasted sweets before.

Back on the bus, Adrian laughs, mouth open and filled with chocolate goop.

"Ew," I squirm, turning away from him. All the while, I'm laughing with my mouth wide open and just as goopy. It was the best damn chocolate bar I'd ever tasted.

After we stuffed our faces, I lean against the seat and, somehow, above all the chatter on the bus, the folklore music in the background, and a screeching child in front, I doze off.

"Issy." A soft voice calls out to me and I open my eyes to find Adrian's face close to mine. "We're here," he says.

I sit up, suddenly alert. "We made it?"

"Yeah."

Thank God. After six hours of climbing up this monstrous garden-of-a-thousand-smells, we made it.

"No. No cars go there." The bus driver unloads our suitcases from the luggage compartment and hands them to us. "Look." He motions to the narrow cobblestone road ahead. "Road too small," he says with his heavy accent and broken English.

"How are we supposed to get there?" Adrian asks.

"Walk."

Adrian stares blankly back at the man. After the nauseating six-hour journey, a brisk uphill walk is the last thing on our agenda. But, if there's one thing I've learned from Adrian, it's to take things in stride and so, with a shrug, I say, "When in Rome, right?"

He rolls his eyes. "What I wouldn't give to have my Beemer right now." Grabbing the handle of his suitcase, he starts walking.

Following the GPS on Adrian's phone, we hike up the incline of the road. Surrounded by fields and trees and rolling hills, the homes are situated far from one another. Many are still in their original form, built of large stones and straw rooftops.

Finally, we arrive at number 2435. In comparison to the old buildings, the cottage is a modern, single-story bungalow built of concrete with a stucco finish. It's painted yellow and has a red-shingled rooftop. Standing on the small square landing, I stare ahead at the decorative carvings on the door.

"Ring the bell," Adrian tells me, but I can't bring myself to do it.

"You're going to get cold feet now?" He reaches around me and presses the doorbell.

A moment later a lean woman appears. She has a

pleasant face and long brown hair. She says something in Portuguese and Adrian politely tells her that we don't speak the language.

"Oh, you're English?" she says with an accent.

"Yes." He answers her with an apologetic smile and goes onto explain that I'm Rachel Pinto's niece.

The woman says she knows Rachel well. "I'm Natalia. Rachel is a wonderful friend to my husband."

When Adrian tells her that I'm Sara Bauer's daughter, the woman's smile vanishes. "Isabella?"

I nod.

With her gaze fixed onto mine, she pulls her black shawl around her shoulders and says, "Please, come inside. I want to show you something."

Adrian and I follow her into a living room of wicker furniture and pastel-coloured pillows. Halting in front of a tall bookcase, Natalia takes hold of a photograph in a silver frame and passes it to me. It's a picture of Eric and Victoria standing on our patio. Mike and I stand next to them, smiling.

Gazing from Natalia back to the photo, I tell her that this photo was just taken this past summer.

Natalia smiles at me. "He kept them all," she says. Turning around, she begins to pull more photographs from the shelves. There's one of my brother and me at our high school graduation, another of my university convocation, and one of Eric in his military uniform.

Then, she hands me an old photo of my brother and me standing on the cobblestone pathway in our backyard, Eric in his bedsheet cape and me with my paper-roll sword. Our new octagon shields are held proudly in front of us.

"He was so happy talking about those days," she says. "I know that he had a good life here with us. He loved us and we loved him." She pauses a moment while tears rise into her eyes. "But I also know that he regretted leaving you and your brother. It was very hard for him."

She shows me another picture. It's the forest behind our house, with the wooden fence, and the cobblestone path partially covered by snow.

"He used to love it when the snow stuck to everything like that. We get lots of snow too, way up here in the mountains," she says with a smile. "I would often catch him sitting out in the yard gazing out at the trees."

Holding the photo in her hands, she gazes down at it. "He missed you and your brother terribly. I would tell him that he should visit, but he would just say that it was not possible. I thought that maybe it was because of the tension with David." She shrugs, "But I think there was something else. He would never speak of it and I did not want to push him."

Natalia sets the photos back onto the shelves. Then, wiping her cheeks, she forces a smile and asks us to follow her into the kitchen.

"He spoke of David often too," she says, placing mugs on the table. "He would tell me many stories." She pauses in thought. "They weren't usually good stories though. Very terrible actually." She laughs as she pours coffee into the mugs.

Adrian laughs along with her, while I force back

tears.

"He was very good to us, your father," she says. "He paid for Patrick's therapy, and the private doctor." She glances up at the ceiling. "He even paid for this home."

"My father?" I'm in awe.

"Yes," she assures me. "They spoke on the telephone sometimes too."

I turn to Adrian whose gaze appears lost in a field of epiphanies.

"He was very generous," she adds. "Patrick would say it was guilt, but I like to think that there was something more to it." Natalia gazes down at her mug and, still smiling, she says, "I am sorry that you did not get to see him. But maybe it is good that you have a picture of him in your mind from those earlier days before he became worse."

I'm saddened by the thought.

Just then, I hear the front door open and I almost gasp at the sight of the tall, broad-shouldered man that soon appears at the entrance to the kitchen.

"Mateo, come," Natalia calls to him. "This is my son."

I stare at the young man unashamed; the resemblance is uncanny. He's tall with blue eyes and sandy blonde hair that showcases a tint of strawberry highlights, and his face - he's a replica of Patrick.

"This is Isabella Bauer," his mother says.

Mateo seems as stunned as I am and, without hesitation, he leans forward and wraps his arms around me.

"You don't know how long I've wanted to meet you,"

he says, his accent milder than his mothers. "My father spoke of you often. He was so proud of you and your brother. He said one day, we would meet." Releasing me, he looks to his mother. "Do you remember that? Do you remember him saying that?"

She smiles and nods. "Yes, I do. He was sure of it."

He turns to Adrian, still smiling. "You must be Eric? The twin?"

"Wish I was but, no, he couldn't make it."

"But you should visit us sometime," I suggest and Mateo's face lights up.

"I would like that very much."

Adrian and I stayed for dinner. They insisted, and I didn't mind. I was happy to stay and listen to more stories of Patrick and their quiet and wonderful life in this small village.

Later, Mateo drove us to the bus stop in his small compact BMW which Adrian boasted about the entire ride. When Mateo and I parted, I felt almost sad to say good-bye.

"I don't get it. She spoke to me last week. So, what changed?"

"The doctor was here this morning," Rachel says over the phone. "It's not good, David."

I grumble at the remark. "We already know it's not good."

"Well, it's worse than we thought."

§

Last week, after they arrived in Europe, Sara and I spoke on the telephone for twenty minutes. She told me that they had settled in, but that Patrick had struggled with the six-story climb up to Rachel and Frank's apartment unit.

"There aren't any elevators? " I asked.

"Not one."

She told me that Patrick was confined to the apartment, escalating an already tense situation. In the background, I could hear the children laughing and screaming.

"How are the children?"

"Oh, they're good." Sara paused to hush them. "But it's hard to keep them quiet. Patrick needs rest, but good luck resting with these two fireballs running around." She huffed in exasperation. "Maybe I'll take them to the beach."

"Sara, love, it's December."

Sara had fallen silent for a moment. Perhaps, the intimacy was too soon. "I know," her voice finally broke through the line. "It's too cold to go into the water, but they can run on the sand."

"Good thinking. Maybe it'll tire them out."

"Yes, maybe." She fell silent once again.

It was good to hear her voice. It was a simple conversation, something we hadn't done in weeks, even if it was a bit awkward. Now, she won't even take my call.

§

"Rachel, you have to get her to talk to me," I say.

"David, you have to understand. It's hard for her to see him suffering like this. He can't stand being treated like a child or an invalid. You know him."

I do know him. Patrick needs to feel useful. "So, that's the reason she won't take my call? What happened with the therapist?"

Patrick was experiencing sharp pains in his head. They began soon after they landed. "He shuts his eyes tight and lays in bed for hours like that," Rachel had told me. Now she says that those sharp jabs may stay with him forever.

"That means he may never be able to drive again. Or work."

After we hang up, I pace. I'd been pacing for days, moving from room to room as though I might find Sara and the twins hiding behind a closed door. But the house remains silent. I know I took it too far. I lost my head - again, and no amount of money or apologies would fix what I had done.

Regardless, I want my family back.

The following week, I call again. This time, I insist on talking to Sara. Rachel tells me to hold on and I can hear them whispering to one another, but I can't make out what they're saying. After two minutes of waiting, Sara answers.

"Hello, David." There's something harsh and formal in her tone.

"When are you coming home?" I ask.

"David -"

"When Sara?"

She was silent for a long while before answering. "I told you."

"I know what you told me, but how are we going to talk properly, or try to resolve anything when you're way over there?"

I'd thought about booking a flight and going to her, but what good would it do? I'd only cause trouble.

Again, Sara hesitates and I ease my tone. "I miss you," I tell her. "And the children. They should be home. They belong here. And you, Sara, you belong here." My voice cracks. "You belong with me."

I can hear a soft whimper on the other end of the line.

"Please, come home."

On a mild December day, I pick up Sara and the twins from the airport. Running out of the airport's sliding doors, Eric and Issy jump into my arms. Sara forces a smile when she sees me, but I can see there's sadness in her eyes.

All the way home, we talk as though nothing had happened. She tells me about Patrick's therapist, a woman named Natalia.

"She got Patrick going up and down those old narrow steps," she says. "This week, he made it all the way down and up again for the first time. But when Natalia first suggested it to him, Patrick said, 'So, you'll carry me back up then?' Natalia laughed about it. They ended up going to a café together so Patrick could rest before going back upstairs again." Sara laughs quietly to herself. "I think he has a crush on her."

"Sounds like he's getting along better than expected."

She shrugs. "Maybe." Her gaze lowers to her lap. "Before Natalia left the apartment yesterday, she asked him if he needed anything. Patrick said he could use a new head."

I turn to look at her and Sara turns her face away, giving the children the chance to jump in. They tell me about the beach and the people surfing in the ocean.

"And they have these men walking on the beach with big boxes of donuts," Eric says. "They're this big." He makes a circle with his little arms. "And they're so good."

Utterly oblivious to the chaos around them, the children adored every moment of the trip. When I ask if they missed being home, they say that they missed their toys. I can't help but laugh.

But, once we arrive at home, things change. Sara spends hours unpacking and organizing and washing. When I try to help her, she tells me that I should spend some time with the children.

At dinner, Sara sets the table while I serve the pasta and meatballs I'd prepared earlier that day, but she doesn't sit with us. Instead, she asks that I tend to Eric and Issy so that she can finish the laundry.

"Are you sure?"

Another forced smile appears on her weary face. "Yes. I'm not hungry right now."

"Sara," I call to her, and she halts half-way out the kitchen door. "You don't have to do laundry today. Stay with us a while."

She looks back at me, her eyes still saddened. "I can't right now."

That evening, I tuck the children into their beds. Eric fusses, insisting he isn't tired while he yawns and snuggles under his comforter.

"Are you sure that you didn't miss your bed?" I ask.

"I miss the beach and the donuts," he says.

Again, I have to laugh at the sweet innocence before moving onto Issy at the other side of the room. The twins insist on sharing a room. They say that it's so they can have the second bedroom as a playroom. Truth of it is, they don't like to be apart, and I wouldn't dare separate them.

"And what do you miss most?" I ask sitting at the edge of Issy's bed.

She reaches up to me and wraps her little arms around my neck. "I missed you, daddy."

I hug her tight. "I missed you too, little girl."

"I miss Patrick too," she says laying her head onto her pillow. "Mommy said he's sick, but he's getting better. That's why we had to go."

"Is that what she said?"

Issy nods and shuts her eyes.

Stepping into our bedroom, I find Sara standing by the bed folding clothes.

"Kids are all tucked in," I tell her.

"Did they give you any trouble?"

"No." A smile comes over me. "Just reminiscing about beaches and donuts."

The corner of her mouth rises and falls again.

"Sara, leave that alone. Come sit with me a while." I reach for her hand and she pulls away.

"I don't want to talk right now. I just want to finish this and go to bed."

The feeling of doubt returns; I wondered how this would end. I'd asked myself if she might ever forgive me, if she'd be able to move on with me or, perhaps, she might choose to go on without me.

"But I do want to say one thing," she utters as she returns to her folding. "What you're doing for him, paying for the therapy, the medication, the doctor," she swallows hard. "It's the right thing to do."

"Sara…" I reach for her once again. "You know I never meant for any of this."

She flashes me a hard look. "Well, that's the problem, isn't it?" She drops the shirt in her hands. "You never mean for any of it, but you do it anyway. You hurt people, David, and you don't think twice about it until it's too late."

"I've never hurt you or the children."

"What you did to Patrick, it hurt us all." Tears fill her eyes. "But it hurt him most, didn't it?"

She turns away and heads towards the door saying, "I'll sleep on the pullout tonight."

"Sara."

She halts at the doorway, and I take a step towards her.

"Do you not want to be married to me anymore? Is that it?" There's an ache in my chest as I struggle to get the words out. "Do you not love me anymore?"

Sara turns to me with a look of astonishment. "How can you say that? David…" She takes a step closer and I watch as the tears run down her cheeks. "I'm in pain because I love you. Because I can't believe that the person I most trust in this world is capable of such brutality. It's unforgivable."

I lower my gaze from hers. She's right. No amount of doctors, therapists, or drugs can ever return Patrick to his former self. This will forever be his new normal, while I carry on with my life.

With a nod, I tell her, "You're right," and drop onto the edge of the bed. "What I did, it's unforgivable. And I know I can't take it back but -" I choke on the words. "God help me - I wish that I could. For his sake, I wish I could take it back. But the thought of him, or anyone else, taking you and the children from me - Sara -" My emotions overwhelm me and, unable to contain them, I lower my head as my eyes cloud over.

Sara moves towards me and I feel her hands slide across my shoulders. "David..." She leans in close and, as though by instinct, I wrap my arms around her waist and lean my face against her.

I can't imagine my life without her and the children, my sweet little children. The thought of it is unbearable. I know in my heart that I need to do everything possible to make things right again. I need to change or risk losing them forever.

"I don't want to lose you, Sara, I can't lose you."

Gently caressing my face, she whispers "You're not going to lose me. I love you too much."

On our final night in Europe, Adrian prepares to head out on an adventure with his new friend, Roberto, the man he'd met on the pier last week.

"Are you sure you don't want to come?" he asks as he stands in front of the mirror fixing his hair. "It's our last night in Europe. We should make the best of it."

Adrian is dressed in dark jeans and a navy t-shirt which makes his skin look even darker than it is. Next to him, I look sickly.

"I'm sure," I reply as I pick up my small carry-on suitcase and toss it onto the bed. "I still need to pack." And I'm too damn exhausted. This trip has left me wanting nothing more than to curl up in a ball and sleep for a week.

I hear the phone ring in the living room and my aunt enters the bedroom with the telephone in her hand.

"Issy," she whispers from the doorway. "It's for you."

From the concerned look on my aunt's face, I'm presuming it's my parents. They've discovered where I am, and they're calling to confront me. I'm not ready for this conversation, but it was bound to occur sooner or later.

When I ask who it is, Rachel covers the telephone receiver and whispers, "It's Eric."

We stare at each other for a second. "How does he know I'm here?" I turn to Adrian, and he shakes his head.

"Don't look at me," he says. "I didn't tell him."

I take the telephone and raise it to my ear. "Eric?"

"What the hell are you doing?" he snaps at me.

"How did you know I was here?"

"Guess."

"I don't know."

"Mom and dad came home to find ten bowls of cat food and water lying around the house. At least you thought to do that much before you f'd off."

"Is this why you called? To scold me?"

"No one knew where you were. Mike said you'd texted him saying you'd be away for a week and that he had to check in on the cat. Why on earth would you leave the key under the doormat? Who does that?"

"Lots of people do that."

"Yeah, people who want to have their home broken

into.”

I huff at him. I don't need this right now. “I'm hanging up.”

“You want to know how I found out where you were?”

I sigh in annoyance. “I'd love to hear it.”

“I called Justin.”

I fall silent.

“Yeah.” There's a hint of sarcasm in his tone. “That's how far I had to go to find you.”

My brother hadn't spoken to Justin in more than two years. Not since the family moved up to Crawford, beyond the Algonquin region. We were all close once until Justin went off to some military school and Eric went to Afghanistan.

“He asked his sister if she knew anything and she told him where you were,” he carries on shouting through the phone. “You go and tell Taylor on the other side of freakin' Ontario, but you couldn't text me?”

“Because you'd try and stop me,” I shout back.

Taylor and I remained close friends. We'd roomed together during University, and we made it a point to keep tabs on each other. Taylor knows everything about me and my chaotic life, just like I know of her struggles in life, and her similarly psychotic brother.

“Let me talk to him.” Adrian's at my side trying to take the phone from me. “I'll explain it.”

“No,” I hiss.

“You're chewing each other's heads off,” he tells me, but I refuse to give up the phone, or the arguement.

“Fine.” Adrian throws his hands in the air and

heads out the door saying, "Don't say I didn't try."

My brother and I quarrel for another five minutes, until he calms down long enough to hear what I have to say. I tell him everything from the photographs I found to the note from Patrick that read, 'Take good care of our babies,' and the conversation with our grandmother that confirmed Patrick's paternity.

My brother had fallen silent.

"Are you still there?" I ask.

"Yeah. I'm here."

"Are you okay?"

"No. This is bullshit. How can they keep this from us?"

"I know." It's hard to accept. "But Patrick has a small cottage up in the mountains," I tell him. "Dad paid for it." I go on to explain that our father has been funding Patrick's medical bills for years, and he continues to send money to Patrick's wife. "And Patrick has a doppelgänger son."

"Are you shittin' me?"

"Nope. We have a brother. He's going to visit us at Christmas."

While my brother tries to get over the shock of the news, I tell him about the concussions that led to Patrick's early death, and Eric falls silent once again. It's another difficult fact to take in.

"That's why they kept it from us. They didn't want us to know what happened between them. I guess they figured we might hate dad for it."

"Hm." That was all that my brother said about it which made me a little uneasy, but I presumed that he just needed time to accept it.

Before we hang up, he's back to himself, jokingly telling me to stop snooping around.

"I don't want to find out next that there's a long-lost triplet somewhere."

I laugh.

"And Issy..." Eric hesitates. "Thank you."

"For what?"

"For everything. For saving me. I've never thanked you before." There's another pause. "So, thank you."

We've haven't talked about the incident since Room B. We'd buried those days and pretended like they never existed. We were both just happy to move forward, not only from those sad days but also from the horrible feelings that they'd left behind.

"You don't have to thank me," I tell him. "You'd do the same for me, right?"

My brother utters a quiet, "Yeah..." and we hang up with hurried goodbye's.

Nearing two o'clock in the morning, I hear the click of the front door. I'm finishing up with my suitcase under the dimmed lighting of the bedside lamp as Adrian sways into the room, smiling.

"Someone had a good time?"

His smile widens. "It was nice."

"Just nice?"

"Okay, I had a blast." He flops onto the edge of the bed. "And why are you still up?"

I shrug. *Folding, thinking, worrying.* I stuff the photograph of Patrick with Natalia and Mateo into one of the side pockets of the suitcase. Natalia had offered it to me as a keepsake. It meant the world to me.

Closing the suitcase, I sit next to him and ask, "Where did you go?"

"To some club. No -" Adrian corrects himself. "Discotheque. That's what they call it. Isn't that cute?"

"Cute? Sure."

"We went with Roberto's crowd. His people, I called them." He laughs and sweeps his hand through his hair and sighs. "At the end of the night, I said, I'll have my people call your people and he said, no." He turns to me with a sultry pout. "No people. You stay here with me."

I laugh. "Stay? Here? Does he know we're leaving tomorrow?"

Adrian is still smiling, "Nope."

"Shouldn't you tell him?"

He falls back onto the bed with his arms spread out and says, "I should, but I can't break his little heart."

"You should have told him," I return to my suitcase, zip it up, and lay it flat on the floor. "He's going to call you tomorrow and discover that you're gone."

"Issy." Adrian grabs my arm and pulls me onto the bed next to him. "You don't get it." He leans close to me and I take in the strong scent of alcohol on his breath. "I'm not going. That's what I'm trying to tell you."

"You're not going where?"

"I'm staying."

I pull back. "You're staying?"

"Yes. Just a week or two."

Clearly, he's drunk because he's making no sense.

"You're telling me that you're going to stay here with this guy who you don't know?"

We sit up and gently, Adrian rests his palms on my cheeks. "It's okay."

"No," I pull away once again. "It's not okay.

"Issy…"

"You don't know this guy. What if he's some creep? What if he tries to hurt you?"

Adrian hushes me, "Roberto is a good guy. He's sweet. He likes me, and I like him. And I can take care of myself."

"Against him and his people, you can't."

Again, Adrian reaches for my face and refuses to let go. "Please, don't be upset."

"I'm not upset," I grumble through puckered lips. "I'm worried."

"You don't have to worry about me."

"Sure, I do. You're my friend. I worry about my friends."

He brushes his hands over my hair and fixes his eyes onto mine. "Honey, the world is not going to fall apart if you stop worrying."

I pause for a moment and let those words sink in.

"I'm going to be fine," he adds. "And you're going home to Mike."

At eight o'clock the following evening, I enter through the front door of my parents' house to find them seated on the sofa in my father's office. Photographs align the table in front of them. As they catch sight of me, they rise together.

"Issy." My mother comes to me with tears in her eyes. "I am so sorry," she says. My father remains where he is, watching me. "Rachel called. She told us what happened. We always meant to tell you."

"It's okay. I'm fine, mom."

I can't tell if they feel bad because I found out or because they kept it from me, regardless, I've already forgiven them. Losing Patrick was hard on them both, as it now is on Eric and me.

Digging into my bag, I pull out the photos I'd taken with me. I give my mother the ones I had found in her room. Then, holding the picture of my father with Patrick from long ago, I step towards my father. "Here, dad." I hand it to him. "This is yours."

He takes it from me, tears rising into his eyes. "I'm sorry that you had to find out this way," he says.

I reach up and hug him. "I'm sorry you lost your friend."

There's nothing left to say about it. It's now in the open and soon, it will become buried in the past, and we will move on from this, together.

As I step through the office door, I look over my shoulder to see my mother place her hands to my father's dampened cheeks, and he lowers his face to hers. The moment brings a smile to my face.

The next morning, I head over to Rosa's Café, now fully renovated since the bombing. I'd heard that the bomb was caused by some angry animal activists and that the lab has since shut down for illegal animal testing.

Sitting at my favourite spot at Rosa's, my notepad

sprawled across the table, I write. I'm almost finished my story, Eric's story. He played a key role in the making of the book, of course, guiding me through it, helping me to understand all the things I couldn't justify and the things I couldn't make sense of.

My error was in my assumptions. For the past two years, I had thought that my brother was on a collision course with death, however, Eric had been trying to come to terms with his place in the world. He had to learn to understand and accept the reason why he was given a chance to live while so many others had died. In the end, it wasn't so much a matter of fate as it was timing.

Had this been one of the Great Wars of 1914 or 1939, would he have made it home to tell us his story? Maybe or, maybe, there is a reason for Eric's place in time. That's what I told my brother. He had a purpose which he'd fulfilled in Afghanistan and he'd returned to tell us his story. Now, his story would continue at the Centre where he would help other veterans tell their stories

As I write, a large figure appears in front of my table, blocking the light from my page. I look up to find Mike staring back at me.

"Hi," he utters with a smile.

"Hi." The butterflies return.

Reaching for the adjacent chair, he asks, "Do you mind if I sit?"

I nod and close the notepad.

"How did it go?" he asks. There's something lighter in his gaze and milder in his tone. Or, perhaps, there's just something different in me.

"You heard?"

He grimaces. "Eric told me. I guess I should have figured something was up when you said you'd be gone a week." He lowers his gaze a moment adding, "I didn't want to pry."

When I texted him, I didn't tell him where I was going, just that I would be gone.

"Thank you for checking in on Tom."

"Of course." He leans in a little closer. "So, what happened? Did you meet him?"

I shake my head and fight against the ache in the back of my throat. "He's gone."

Mike's face falls. "Gone?"

I nod, speechless.

"I'm so sorry."

I knew from the start that there was a good chance that I might not find Patrick. I hadn't expected that he would be gone, of course, but the possibility that I may never see him had always been there. The fight from long ago and the secrecy of his past gave it away. I supposed, in the back of my mind, I'd always expected this to be the outcome.

"It's incredible how the mind will block things out or force them right back in again, isn't it?" my aunt had said.

Tears fill my eyes. Since the visit to Patrick's cottage that day, I'd kept the idea of him in the back of my mind, tucked away where it was safe. Now, reality setting in, twenty years of wondering was over, and I allowed my emotions to take over. I wish so much that things could have ended differently.

With an arm around my shoulders, Mike suggests that we get some air. I pick up my things and we head out towards the lakeshore.

"You know, despite the heartache, I'm glad you did this," he says as we cross the road. "I'm glad that you found what you were searching for."

"Yeah, me too." As much as it hurts, I'm thankful for the resolve.

"And you removed the bandages," he says.

I look down at the scars left behind.

"Don't worry," he says. "That'll heal too."

We walk in silence for a moment, until we reach the lake. Then, turning to face me, Mike says, "I'm sorry I've been such an asshole."

The comment is unexpected, although, I know it's not all on him. I had a big part in the mess that we had created for each other.

Taking my hands into his, he utters, "You know, in Ottawa, when I asked you to marry me, I meant it."

I don't know what to say to him... I never wanted us to fall apart, but it seemed natural that we should fall while the world crumbled around us. Perhaps our reality had become too difficult, and life had just become too damn hard.

We hadn't been ready to face the reality of losing a best friend, a brother, nor were we equipped to understand how to keep him alive. How do you convince someone to love themselves? But things had changed, things are still changing.

I rest my forehead against his chest, and Mike's

arms wrap around me and press me close to him.
"And I meant it when I said, yes."

Chapter 30   December 1996

The next morning, the sun is shining into the bedroom through the open drapes. I turn to see Sara lying asleep at my side, her hair sprawled across the pillowcase, her shoulders exposed. I reach out to her...

"Daddy. Daddy." The children run into the bedroom and jump up onto the bed shouting. "Wake up. Wake up."

"Okay, okay," I laugh. "I'm up."

"Go downstairs," Sara tells them with a hand pressed to her forehead. "Get your cereal out and we'll be right down."

As the children stomp down the stairs giggling, I turn to Sara. My hand reaches across her shoulders and comes to rest on her back. "Jetlag?" I ask.

"Ugh, yes," she groans with a smirk.

"We'll get you something for that downstairs."

She nods, and I pull her close. "But this does feel right, doesn't it?"

Sara touches her hand to my face.

In the kitchen, we prepare breakfast for the twins. Looking across at Sara, I feel that she's happy. I pass by her and kiss her on the cheek. She smiles back at me. I think she's happy.

After breakfast, the twins hurry to get their bedsheet capes. I fasten them around their shoulders and hand them their fortified swords and shields.

"There you go, Sir Eric and Lady Isabella. You are now ready to battle the evil serpent."

They rush outside in their snowsuits. Laughing and screaming excitedly, they chase after one another, leaping over the cobblestone pathway partially buried by the snow.

This moment, it will forever be engraved in my mind. I will never forget who made them, but they will never forget who raised them.

Sara and I stand watching the twins from behind the French doors. I wrap my arm around her, and she leans into me.

"This does feel right," she whispers.

She presses her lips to mine and the warmth of her touch makes me smile.

Acknowledgments

There is an army of people who have helped me along this incredible journey. From my patient professor, Guy Allen, at the University of Toronto, to my editor's, Deborah Ferdinand and Angie Athanasakos, of Creative Consulting Services Inc. Thank you for your guidance, your knowledge, and your ongoing support.

Thank you to my talented cover designer, Katherine Mountford for her wisdom with designing my cover page, and to Michael Hills of Mike Hills Photography for his inspirational and beautiful photograph.

I would also like to thank my family for their continued support and thank you to Cristina Correia for her aid throughout this project.

And a special thank you to my copyeditor, Katie – my angel, who worked with me through all of the bumps and hurdles. Without you, I don't know how I could have made it to completion. Thank you for keeping me on track.

www.ingramcontent.com/pod-product-compliance
Lightning Source LLC
Chambersburg PA
CBHW030903060726
47591CB00005B/1395